The Ghastling

"SPRING"

The Ghastling

TALES OF GHOSTS, THE MACABRE AND THE OH-SO STRANGE

EDITOR
Rebecca Parfitt
GRAPHIC DESIGNER
Andrew Robinson
EDITORIAL ASSISTANT
Tracey Rees
SOCIAL MEDIA MANAGER
Jen Smith-Furmage

SPECIAL THANKS
Hannah Durham
J&C Parfitt

CONTACT
editor@theghastling.com
theghastling.com
Social Media: @*TheGhastling*

PUBLISHED BY THE GHASTLING

The Ghastling gratefully acknowledges the financial support of the Books Council of Wales.

ISSN: 2514-815X
ISBN: 978-1-8381891-8-1

Contents

Editorial *by Rebecca Parfitt*

Dear reader,

As 2024 marks the 10th anniversary of *The Ghastling*'s existence, a decade of hauntings and horrors is much to celebrate. It started as an online magazine, which was too beautiful not to print, and now we have released one short 'episode' in audio of Alex Gillinder's tale 'Dead Stories' which featured in book 18, if you haven't had a listen yet, please do, it's available for free on *Patreon.com/TheGhastling*. We are hoping to produce more audio episodes over the next year.

At the beginning, we were one of a handful of magazines publishing short fiction of this kind, but now we are one of many and the last decade has certainly seen a resurgence in the interest in the ghost story — and horror in all its forms — as a genre to be taken seriously. It is so exciting to see it thriving. But why? The world is a scary place and we have much to be worried about in our everyday realities. And sometimes worry and threat manifests itself in our consciousness and the product of our creative endeavours can be deliciously unsettling. Writing or reading horror can sometimes feel like a therapeutic and diverting way of coping with the anxieties of life. What is it about horror and ghost stories that is so addictive? Well, for me, it's a genre that can sneak into the room with you unlike any other... wait, what is that standing behind you?

Boo!

I would like to welcome our new graphic designer, Andrew Robinson. Andrew is no stranger around these parts, his illustrations have featured in several previous issues and we are very excited to see what he does with the magazine.

All of the stories here contain an element of transformation and change; hauntings, the uncanny, folk horror and strange creatures also lurk amongst the pages. A ghostly hitchhiker forces a lonely traveller to question all that is real in **Mat Troy**'s thought-provoking story, 'Nancy'.

Living by a remote moor, disillusioned by play-groups and the education system, Frankie decides to home educate her young children, but the task of parenting becomes relentless— too relentless. So Frankie, having consulted a grimoire, finds another truly petrifying way to cope. In **Charlotte Turnbull**'s folk horror, 'Sharing Stone'.

A mother and her 14-year-old daughter live alone in a remote house. The mother must leave her daughter while she goes off to work night shifts; one day three strands of horse-hair appear on the mother's pillow and strange hoof tracks in the snow encircle the house in this truly eerie tale, 'Five Knocks' by **Fawn Emmalee Ward**.

Two housemates think the other is the perpetrator of strange noises in the attic. Their neighbours, too, are suspicious. A beautifully creepy and subtle exploration of what might haunt us in **Ashley Harnett**'s, 'It Was Nothing'.

A house-bound and miserable man starts to notice a peregrine falcon is terrorising and killing the pigeons that visit him in his block of flats. He soon realises there's a lot more to gain from feeding the birds in **Simon John Parkin**'s 'Peregrination'.

A woman receives the news that someone very dear to her has been found dead. Grief-stricken and unable to comprehend the news, she does what she would normally do: heads to the swimming pool - she was going anyway. As she swims, she starts to hear something recognisable, yet very strange, in the water. In **Katherine Stansfield**'s, 'The Call'.

Ever been to a house viewing and wondered who'd lived there before and what happened to them? One prospective tenant is given a viewing that haunts them long-after in **Alex Gillinder**'s, 'The Viewing'.

The son of a wealthy baron returns to the home he would rather forget. But unfortunately it seems his dead wife walks again and something must be done, in **Emma Oxley**'s tale of the unquiet dead, 'The Return.'

Eight tales to keep you up at night, settle in, and make sure you are very much alone...

Thank you for reading! Every sale helps us to continue producing this magazine.

Best wishes,
Rebecca Parfitt
Editor, *The Ghastling*

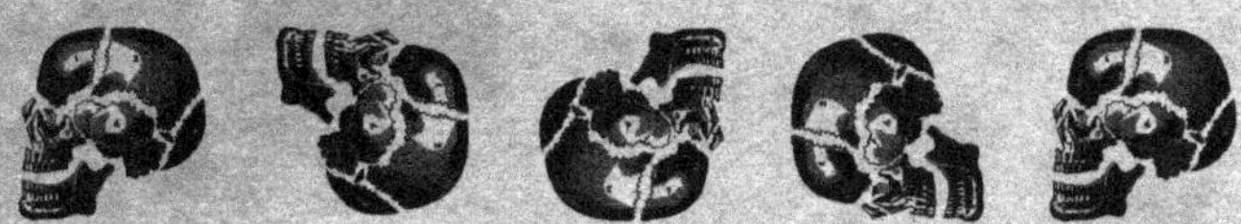

The Ghastling wishes to
RECOGNISE
our most distinguished
PATRONS
of the Headless Horseman

(L-R) DEMETER, PAMELA KOEHNE-DRUBE, MARTHA, WYN LEWIS, BRAD SINGER

"PROTECT THE CHILD"

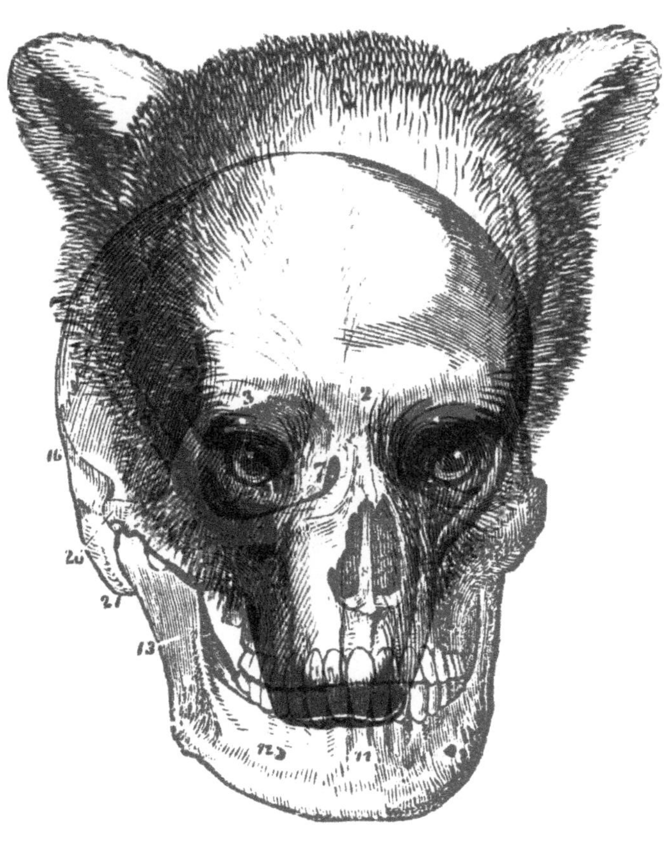

Five Knocks

by Fawn Emmalee Ward

The morning that my mother found the horse hairs on her pillow was bitingly cold.

HER water glass on the bedside table skimmed over gently with fragments of ice in the dull winter light.

I knocked on the wall in my room, hitting the repeating rosette in the wallpaper with my knuckle. Five gentle knocks, *are-you-a-wake-yet*? A long pause, then one soft knock *yes* in return. Our secret language from room to room. I slid out from under my heavy blankets. We shared a wall, but the walk from door to door took me down the hallway and across the long kitchen into the mudroom where the cellar stairs sloped down below and around the corner behind the coat closet. Strange design for a house, my mother said. Bedrooms that shared a wall but took fifty steps to walk between. We knocked back and forth, counting taps for meaning.

I pushed her door open carefully. She sat up in bed, covers across her legs. I climbed next to her and looked down at the pillow in her arms. Three long black hairs stretched out across the faded case.

'Horse,' she said, the *s* catching in her throat.

I ran my finger down the length of them. Mane hair, glossed and round. She shook her head, frowning.

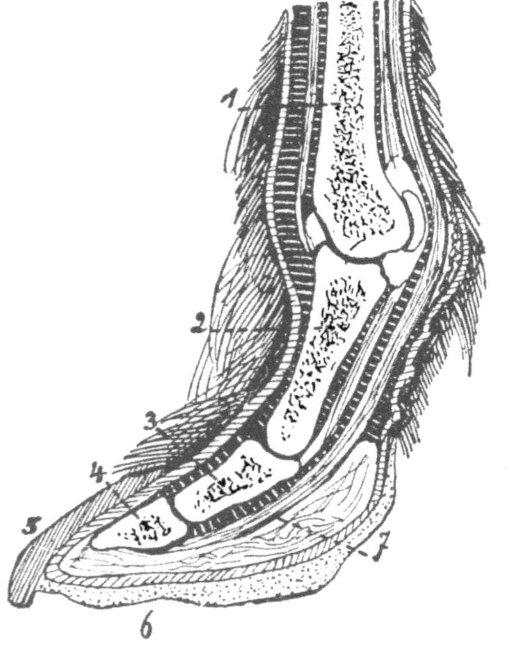

'Where did they come from?' I asked. She met my eyes in silence. We had no horses here

This was before she started working nights, leaving me after dinner for the hour and a half drive into town.

'You're 14 now. You can take care of yourself for a little while,' she said, smoothing her hands over my braids, little sandy-blonde strays popping out the sides.

We were caretaking an old house in the foothills above town for winter — far from everything, but it was what we could afford after my mother's boyfriend had kicked us off his ranch at the beginning of fall. I could still taste the dust of oats and hay, the lanolin-smoothed saddle smells. The soft sweetness of the appaloosas' breath as they bit a summer apple from my hand. Our boots and leathers now shoved in a black garbage bag and thrown to the back of the closet; I still had not unpacked most of my things.

I watched my mother walk down the driveway with her flashlight toward the truck at the gate where the road got plowed. Every night after she left, I moved through the house turning on light after light. I didn't want to let in the darkness outside too close. Before bed I would turn the lights off one by one, retreating backwards to my own room.

The knocks were quiet at first and I mistook the sound for the wind brushing boughs along the gutter. But it kept on. I opened my eyes to moonlight. Five knocks.

Are-you-a-wake-yet? Silence.

Five knocks. *Are-you-a-wake-yet*?

I held my ear to the wall, measuring the sound. My mother's hand was small and delicate-boned. This sound was heavy; held an unfamiliar weight. I looked over to the neon clock: 3:27. My breath was fast as I stared at the rosettes glowing from the brightness of the moon. My mother wouldn't be home until six.

Five knocks.

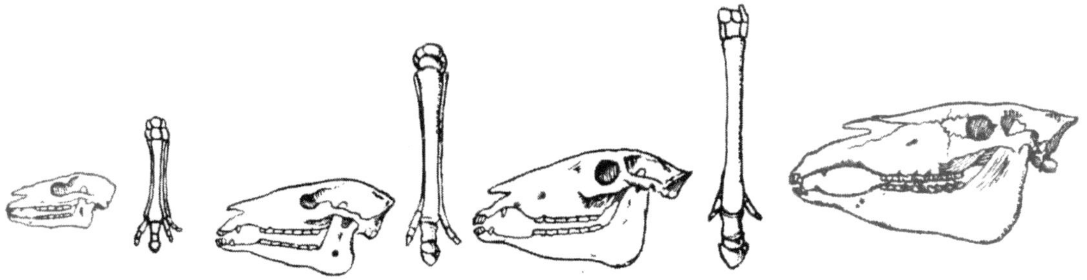

I shuffled out of the room, opening my door to a flood of bright lamplight. Blinking, I stumbled down the hall. I had turned the lights off before bed; I was sure of this.

I approached the mudroom and paused, a chill rustling over my face. The front door was wide open into the darkness. I looked around wildly on the stoop, grabbing at the freezing brass knob. Nobody was out there only night.

I tiptoed back to my room and counted myself to sleep. No more knocks.

When I awoke, my mother was already home, making tea on the kitchen stove. She ruffled my messy hair and pulled the scarf tighter around her neck. I'd long let the fire run cold overnight, and we didn't bother rekindling during the day now since all she did was sleep.

I walked to the school bus, waving lightly to her figure in the window, a slight, pale woman in the shadows clutching her steaming cup. The moon had sunk back behind the spiny trees, so I mostly saw the glowing yellow kitchen lights orbing around her in the still-dark not-quite-night.

She was awake again when I returned. 'I have to show you something,' she said, meeting me at the door in her boots. I dropped my pack.

'What is it?' I asked, stifling a yawn. The light outside was already dim and my eyes struggled to open wide.

She stopped suddenly at the corner of the house. 'Here.' She pointed a bare finger to the ground. I stooped to see. Prints — large enough

I had to shift my gaze to take them fully in. Four toes and three little lobes on the back. I held my hand above and it was the same size.

My mother continued, walking around the prints so as not to disturb their mark. 'See, more here,' she said, gesturing. I looked where she was. These were at least six feet from the last print, in pairs.

'Cougar?' I asked. Mountain lions step into their own prints in snow, obscuring half the evidence of their paths.

She nodded slowly. 'Maybe. I've never seen them so far apart before. It must have been huge.'

'Where do they go?' I asked, sniffling into the cold late afternoon air. She kept walking. I shoved my big feet into her smaller tracks, slipping on the compacting snow. Obscuring half the evidence of us, here.

'All the way around,' she said, out of breath. 'All the way around the house. It looks like they start and stop here —' She pointed in front of the door. I shivered. A few new snowflakes settled down toward the ground. My mother grabbed my hand, rubbing it warm.

I sat on her bed as she got ready for work after dinner. The snow had picked up, so she had to leave early to navigate the slippery county road. She brushed her silvering hair and looked into a tiny mirror atop her dresser next to the dark horse hairs she'd laid out.

'You're going to be fine,' she said without turning around.

I looked up. 'Yeah,' I said. 'So will you.'

She smiled.

The falling snow erased all but a smudge of her flashlight as she made new prints toward the road and in an hour you wouldn't see them at all.

I pulled a blanket over me, the one I'd taken from my room at the ranch, woolen edges ratty and coarse.

'Go pack everything,' my mother had said the night we left. 'You still have your boxes.' Our long-used cardboard, covered in crossed-through marker notes: *summer clothes, books, toys + dolls.*

I'd moved slowly at first, folding things carefully into the tattering cartons until I heard the yelling from their room. Keepsakes and fragiles dumped right in next to heavy things, it all went together then.

I wrapped the blanket around my ears; I didn't want to hear anything.

'Are you awake yet?'

My mother stood over me, a cool hand on my hair. I sat up, sucking in the chilled air.

'What time is it?'

'A little after six,' she said. 'Time for school.'

It was too cold to shower, so I splashed water across my face and stood staring blankly in the bathroom's dull light, my eyes suddenly wide. Something was not right.

I stepped outside into the hallway in the dark and I heard her scream.

Fifty steps from door to door, I stumbled through the rooms in the dim to find her. Down the kitchen's scuffed linoleum, tripping over winter boots by the cellar door. In her bedroom, my mother stood holding her hands on the big window's frame.

'Look,' she said, her voice a faint hush.

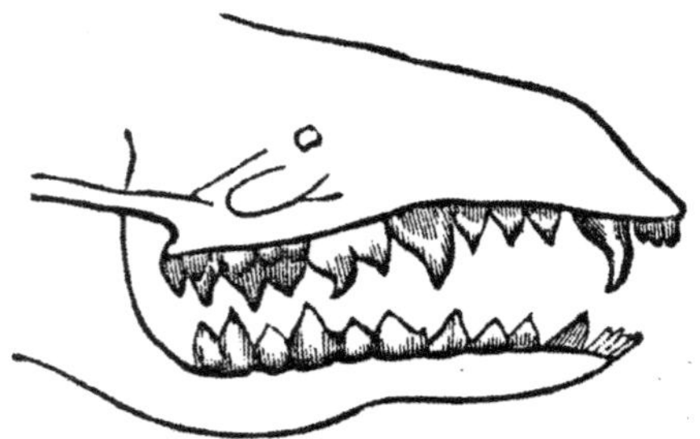

I focused outside into the darkness and slowly a shape came into view. Blinking, I felt my heart rise.

A large animal crouched by the fence, looking back at us. The body of an enormous mountain lion formed out of the darkness, its fur bristling lightly in the still-falling snow. I blinked in disbelief as I saw its silhouette rising sharply from a muscled cat's shoulders into the long, dark-framed line of a horse's head, dark mane tossed to one side. It took several steps toward the window and I gasped, folding myself backwards away from the windowsill. My mother did not budge. She didn't look away as it turned its long head to the side so the whiteless eye could stare in; she was not afraid. I trembled there.

'It's okay,' my mother whispered. 'It will leave, or we will.'

I held my breath and found my voice again. 'I don't want to leave,' I said. 'We always have to leave.'

She nodded and grabbed my hand. We stood there, we would stand there for as long as it took, both of us staring the strange beast down until the violet morning light seeped across the yard, inching toward its massive limbs.

Slowly it raised a snowy paw and tapped up at the glass. Five knocks. It stared back at us.

Carefully, I reached a cold finger up to the glass. *Yes*, we are, we are here.

The school bus never came that day, though I watched for it from the window. The snow was too deep to drive up the county road and the plow hadn't come. I laid in bed with my sleeping mother, sharing the little warmth we could generate together in the house's freezing winter air.

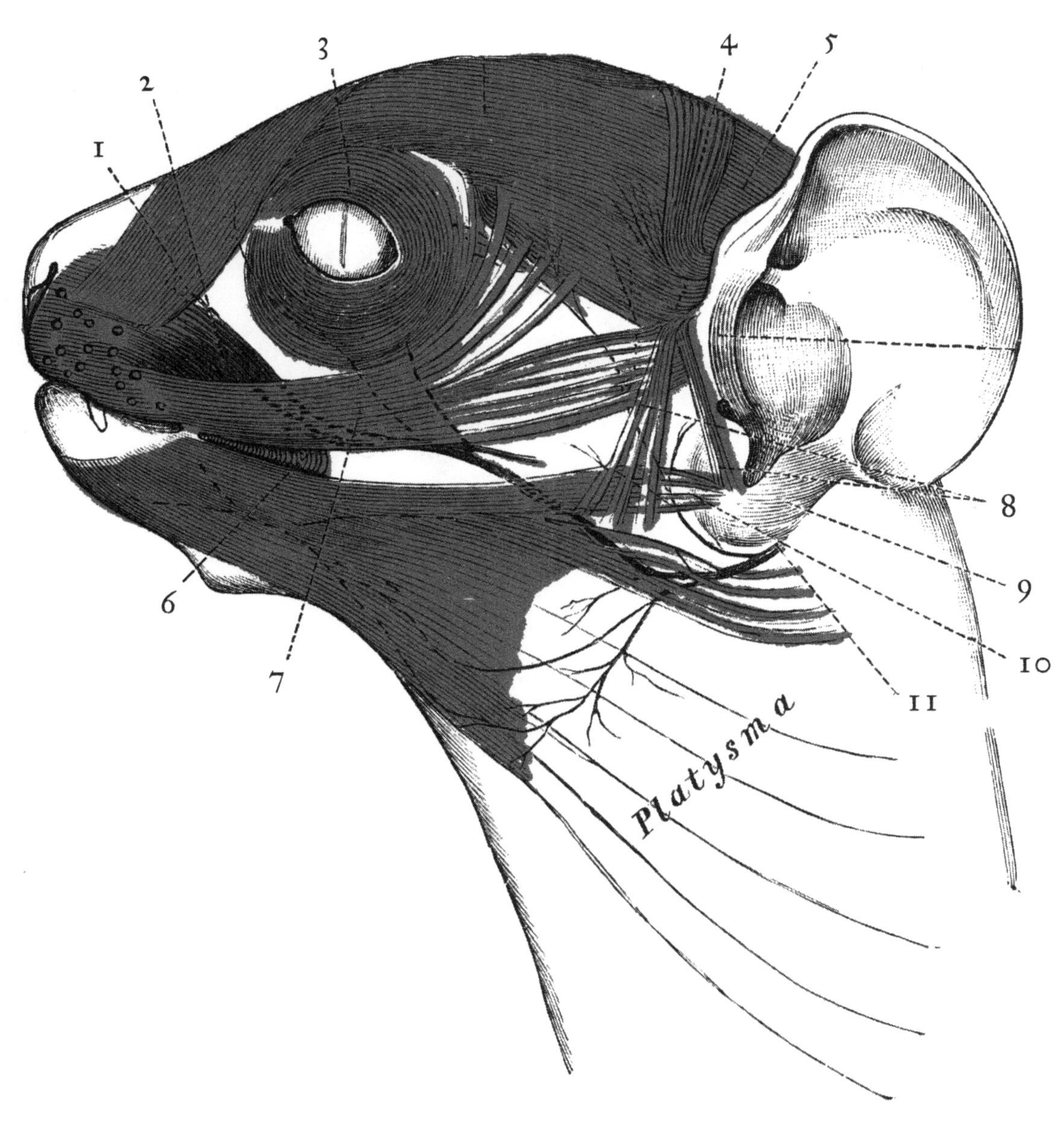

1
2
3
4
5
6
7
8
9
10
11
Platysma

THE NEW BUDGET OF RECITATIONS.

A HUMAN DEVIL; OR, THE BITER BIT.

Sharing Stone

by Charlotte Turnbull

The village hall looked like a cage. There were bars outside the windows, but inside it was staged like a living room. A sofa and rug had been placed in the middle of too large a space.

THE women crowded in as close as possible, dovetailing with soft furnishings. The rest of the room was an empty rectangle of pale floorboards and hard angles. Just waiting for a child to slip and split a lip on.

Frankie thought her son might like to socialise, but now her jaw hardened as she sank into the sofa — eyes greying and flecked with crystals watching the boy play without her.

A health visitor trickled among them, only interested in physical milestones; whether a child's thumb and index finger met in a pincer; what they would, or wouldn't eat.

'There's coffee,' the health visitor said. 'I'm not here to judge.' The empty room cast her final word around the walls, again and again.

'Are we the shy, weak ankle of feminism?' Frankie laughed, but the other women looked at her blankly. 'Or the heroic, thick calf?' she said, quietly, apologetic.

They turned away.

'Tony says I have nice calves,' said the mother next to her.

On the floor, in the middle of the rug, someone sat down to feed a newborn and Frankie tried to remember the last time she'd seen her husband.

'Tony sounds nice,' Frankie said, and the other mother smiled, relieved.

As they stared at the feeding baby, it unlatched. Those on the sofa were misted with sweet milk, sanctified by the swinging censer of breast.

'My son's so curious, I don't know whether other children will like it,' Frankie said to anyone.

Someone pushed him over.

'They work it out,' a woman perched on the arm of the sofa replied mysteriously, leaving her own children to the red-eyed scrum of nature and looking the opposite way, out of the window, beyond the bars, where it had started hailing. 'It's one big game.'

Her baby scrambled up, someone kicked him.

She waited for someone to do something but sleep glimmered, shifting and contorting sight like the aura of a migraine. She did not blame them. They all placed glamours upon their words so they would sound broad and benevolent — like *mothers*. But underneath it she felt the white-knuckled grip on whatever they could keep hold of for themselves — recreating was, after all, an inherently selfish act.

The boy was crushed beneath four or five of them, when Frankie suddenly realised her son was nothing but a fragile brew of water and electricity.

She stood up from the sofa. The women sitting either side of her crashed into one another.

She pulled the boy out, swinging heavily around. A new sibling clung on inside her belly as she took the straps of her floral oilcloth changing bag in a fist.

Children were asked 'What happened?' Children were told 'Say sorry'. Her son had a shocked look on his face.

No, she thought, not this.

They stopped doing toddler groups.

The school had a secure entrance system. There were alarms, and codes, and metal detectors, and special temporary passes printed with your name, address and purpose of visit, but eventually Frankie was allowed into the lobby.

On a noticeboard entitled 'Reception Portraits' nostrils and ears loomed large, but eyes were tiny, with lashes crooked as spider legs. Her boy had drawn a smiling sun with eight yellow arms, a yellow hand at the end of each.

'Where is his father?' The head did not approve of flexi-schooling, seated adult-height at his adult's desk in his adult's office.

'It's not that simple,' she said, imagining smashing her own nose against the low child's table in front of her. She stroked the hair of the baby wrapped into her chest.

'We don't feel the need to get him assessed,' the head said, which made her wonder if there was a need to get him assessed. 'School is great for consistency.'

She decided to home-school, where her son

never had to sit still for long periods of time. They made stick hedgehogs and pebble families. They sang about Green Besoms and Widecombe Fair. They learned the properties of plants and lunar phases.

By three years old, the little girl was already finishing her brother's sentences. That autumn she saw them whisking a stick about in the leat at the bottom of the garden.

'Don't lean too far out,' Frankie shouted, running for the little one. 'Don't fall in.'

They showed her a horse chestnut case they'd seen bobbing past in the water. Inside were three shining conkers, each crushed but growing around the others. Ritual came easily to the children. It was all they'd ever known — in their kitchen a grimoire was pressed open where once it had been *Easy Finger Foods* — so they held the spiky green shell together, lifting it to their 'sharing stone' in the garden. It was a huge rock, tall as a man. They used its shade for picnics in the summer. In winter, Frankie used it on nights when her husband came home. On nights when she needed to breathe wild air. When she craved the soft kiss of silt between her toes, but wanted the unbreakable at her back.

One day Frankie took the children to the park. She kept her eyes low. There was a bench stuffed with other mothers, but they all avoided each other. No one had the energy. They scrolled through the news on their phones, flooding themselves with adrenaline, murder and abuse.

Her son circled a plastic horse bouncing on a huge spring, waiting patiently for a turn. One child got off, and another child crossed the field, fast, to get on. The child pushed her son out of the way and leapt on, flung the horse back and forth — so fast its eyes seemed bloodied and its teeth seemed black. Her daughter caught the toy by its head, plunging it down towards the grass, tipping the child forward until they could do nothing but cling on.

'Let my brother have a go,' she said.

Frankie looked around, saw another mother watching and winced — *sorry*.

But she was relieved. She wanted her daughter's bones dissolved until only the rock of her remained: not for her, the fear of dislike, or the misery of a manipulative compliment.

She took her children, one by each hand, yet another new babe bellied in between and went home.

Her neighbour took the children next door when Frankie went into labour.

Afterwards, they entered the living room quietly, trying to whisper when she introduced them to their new brother, black-eyed and still covered in curd.

'Put it on the table.' The girl pushed crayons and paper to the floor.

Frankie laughed. She didn't want to wait — the children were perfect as they were — but she wanted time with the newborn, so she left it a few more weeks.

One morning she took them to walk in the trees by the leat, to see the hoar feathering the leaves. The infant was bound upon her chest, as they threw pebbles into the black water. The eldest dredged out three rocks: one biggest, one middlest, one littlest.

'Am I the water?' Frankie asked him.

The boy had no idea what she was talking about. He was barely seven.

They took the rocks and did a project. Her son learned granite doesn't erode.

"Mountins are made of it," he wrote on his poster stuck to the fridge door. "It is so strong and assidic it EATS other rocks. We see it at the surfice because it surfifes when other rocks crumbl away."

She didn't sleep. She didn't eat. She worked for the family all the time. Passion flowers picked under pink skies. Mushrooms stewed into tea. She chanted to noctule bats. She nursed a leveret. Out on the moors, it was a bartering circle of giving and taking.

But at home, she was only giving, giving, giving.

She never saw the other witches, but she knew they were there; crushed cotton flowers. Twig sigils in moonlit glades —

— the scent on her husband's breath.

At six weeks, the little baby pricked his cheeks with dimples for the first time.

She had to spare him the rest, end it while he was innocent, happy.

She washed their faces, brushed their hair, dressed them in their favourite clothes.

'Smile,' she said. The boy raised his hand to his face, fending her off — she caught him by surprise.

The hexes were stretching in Frankie's aorta; magma cruising through her veins.

His sister realised what had happened and turned, eyes narrow and accusing. Now, her stone finger would always point at her mother, but Frankie couldn't have stopped changing them even if she'd wanted to.

She took the baby from its crib, and lay it at their feet; little bald head so smooth and new. Its arms outstretched to her, forever. Like Medea, she thought, I fell in love.

Afterwards, she sat in the living room with her stone ornaments cradling the fireplace. Youngest in the middle, bigger ones either side. She could drink tea while it was still hot, read a book to the end, and there they were, exactly as she'd left them.

No one coming home crying from school — no one coming home laughing either.

It was bliss, for a few weeks.

Then she noticed her toes going, the soft tissues between them ossifying: a side effect she had not expected.

After all that, she had to be sure they'd stay together.

The woman who lived next door helped her load them into the car. The woman's sons watched for a while, then began to shoot each other with wands made of twigs, miming explosions, falling stiff like the statues to the ground wailing.

' — that isn't how it was,' she told the woman, as they watched the boys' game. The woman smiled and shrugged.

Frankie tightened the seat belts against their stone bodies. Booster seats cushioned them on the track up to the moor. She found a spot away from other stone circles and stone rows, so they could become their own site-of-interest.

She carved little soil beds to tuck them in, so they would stand solid in the full slap of the weather.

In a crook of gorse for shelter, she set up her husband's old tent and laid a fire. She hung a heavy cast iron pot that would not blow away in the wuthering, and slept each night in the shadow of a collapsed tor.

While she could still move, she would clean away their lichens and liverworts each week. Then one morning she noticed the webbing between her fingers springy with moss.

Even in the rain and hail it was easier to keep her eyes open with her lids so gritty, and she could see all of them at once if she stared straight ahead at the drift of the moor.

She was almost completely petrified when a young woman with a map approached them. Frankie's eyeballs growled in their sockets, following the woman as she wove between the three perfect, little statues.

The woman bent down to press the summer burst of bedstraw back, to see the feet of the older ones, to tug out the grass tickling the babe's sides. She stood up and looked at the tripod blown into the gorse, at the blackened turf where the fire had been. She ducked down, peering into the tent — door still flapping in the breeze where Frankie hadn't been able to grip the zip.

The woman pulled her heel up against the back pocket of her shorts, grabbing the walking boot behind her to stretch the front of one thigh, then the other.

Frankie sighed to see blood thump beneath pink skin on the hot day. The woman flinched, then leaned in close, swatting the map at a fritillary that had settled upon Frankie's stone nose.

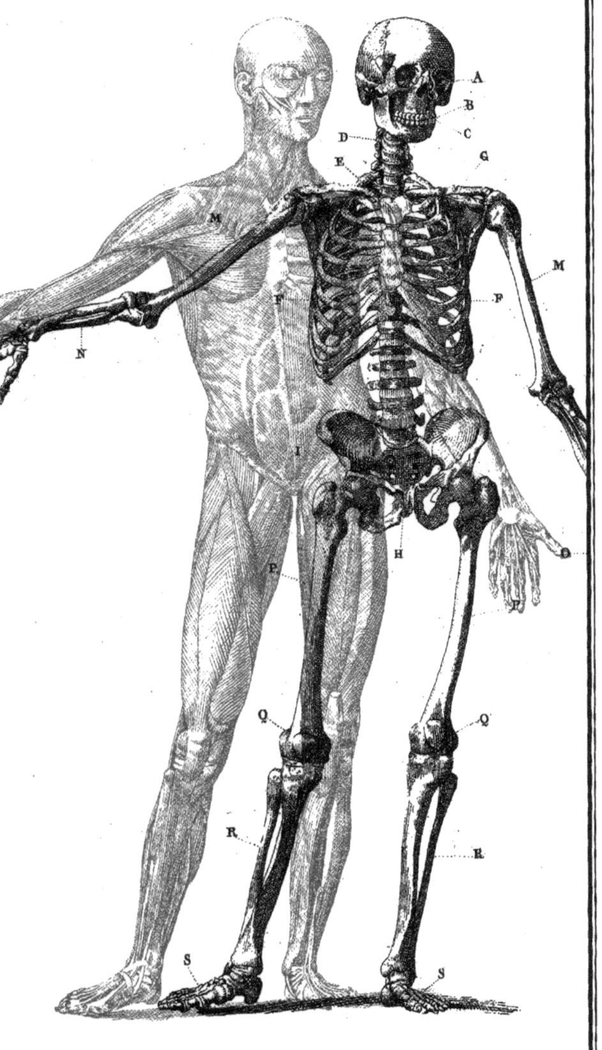

'It's only the three children on the map,' said the woman.

'It's usually spinsters or maidens,' Frankie rasped, her tongue tabled stone. The woman looked at her, trying to take her meaning. Frankie's hands — phalanges, metacarpals, carpels — were fused into one and now, finally, she had claws.

'But where,' said the woman, her own eyes flashing a little grey, 'is their father?'

'It was nothing to do with us,' Frankie said, too quickly.

He was never like them. He wasn't granite but limestone – brittle since the day she'd met him. The last she'd heard, shortly after the littlest was born, they'd moved him inside from the beer garden for fear of frost shattering.

'Visit him, if you like,' Frankie said, 'Ask for the statue in the bar of the Ring O' Bells.'

The woman folded her map, rolled her shoulders and walked away.

When the weather was nice, her neighbour brought the boys with a picnic.

She sat at Frankie's feet, rested her head against Frankie's knees, eyes closed in the sun, just for a little while.

Frankie kept an eye on the boys while they played with her children, holding their hands, hanging off their backs, kissing the baby's head. She wished she could smile.

Sometimes the neighbour brought news.

'Your man's head came off,' she said one Sunday afternoon. 'Broke the landlord's foot. He's wrapped in a tarp in their shed now.'

In the winter the wind kicks like a ball from one side of the moor to the other and Frankie doesn't so much as shiver — the boy's hand doesn't flinch — the girl's finger never falters — but sometimes, although she tries not to hear, it sounds exactly like a baby crying.

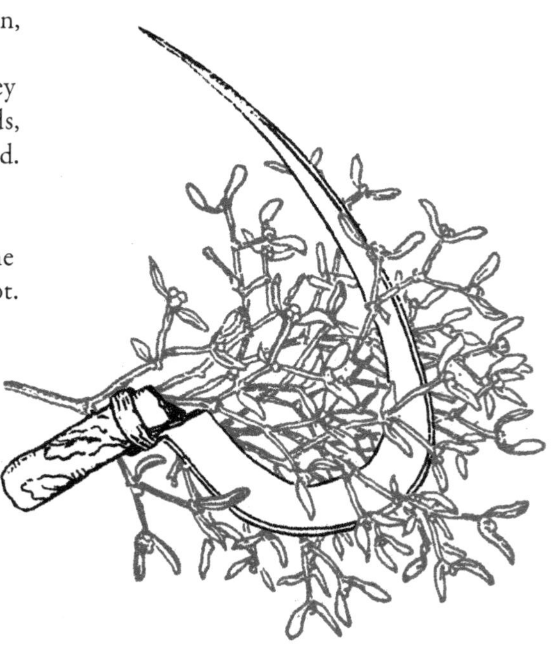

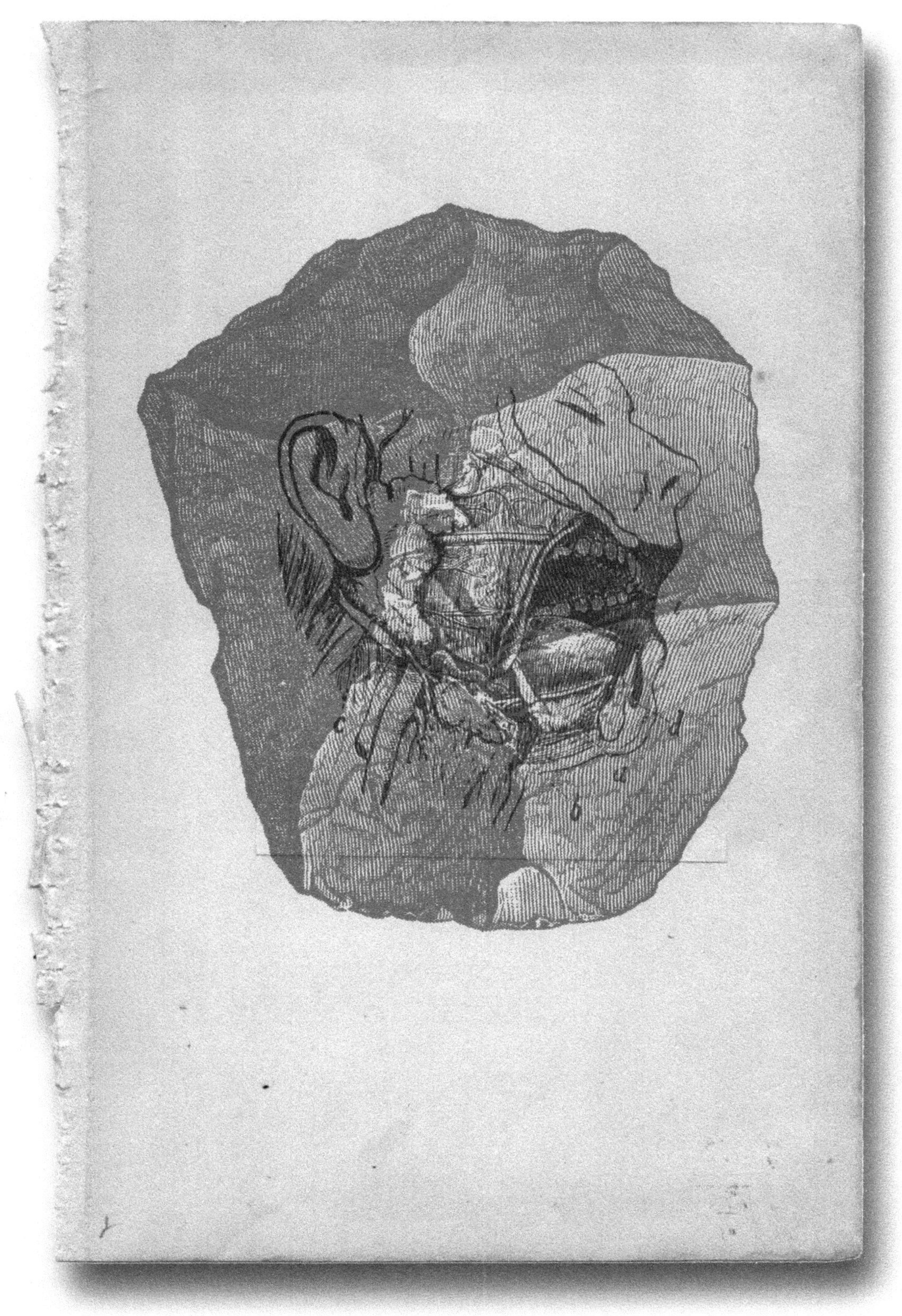

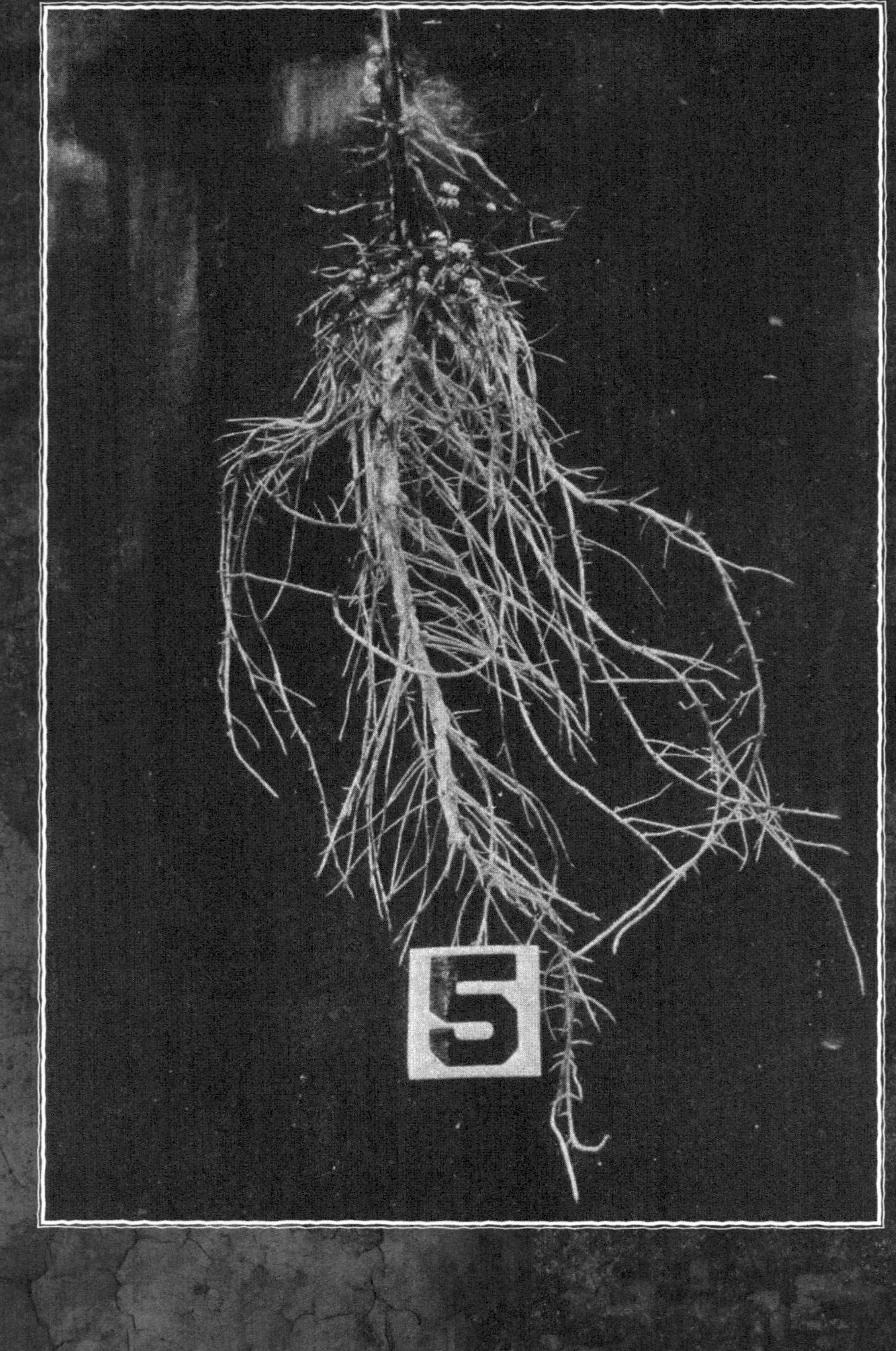

5

The Call

by Katherine Stansfield

I hung up the phone and decided I would still go for a swim. My stuff was already in the bag and I'd had my keys in my hand when the phone rang so I didn't have to think about it, which was something.

THAT makes it sound as if I just hung up and went straight out the door. At first, that's what I thought I'd done. But when I reached the changing rooms I realised that I must have stayed in the house longer than I'd thought because the aquafit ladies had all packed up and gone. Not a single one of them still at the hairdryers, putting their curls back in. Usually I arrive just as they're getting in the showers after their class and the pool has emptied out, and then by the time I've finished my swim, the changing room is quiet again. But that day I arrived to the quiet, and it was a bad quiet. Too much.

In that quiet I realised I couldn't remember anything that happened after the call. I guess I just stood there in the hall which is where I'd been, keys in hand, reaching for the lock, the handle of my swim bag looped over my other wrist, when the call came. Or maybe I sat on the sofa for a while and I forgot about it. I could have been outside the house, just staring at the car, or sitting in the car outside the house, or in the car in the pool's car park.

Carrying on, going for the swim, it made sense as a thing to do next because people can't tell if you're crying in the pool, but of course I didn't think about the changing room and the toilet cubicle and the shower before you get in. I cried in all those places, and by the time I was ready to get in the water, after all that crying, there were people around again, making use of the lull after the aquafit class, like me.

And then once I was in the water, my goggles filled with tears so I had to keep stopping to empty them. Managing my breath was harder than normal as well. I'm usually pretty good at that, with breaststroke at least, but that day I was all out of sync, spluttering, near choking a few times, and because I had my ear plugs in, I couldn't tell how loud I was, the sobbing and the choking. But with the goggle situation I couldn't see anyone looking at me anyway so I kept on as best I could and I managed twenty-seven lengths so not far off my regular goal.

But it didn't distract me the way I'd hoped. It didn't stop me thinking.

It could have been so much worse. Not to know. This is why you get the chip, I realised. It's not just for the stories about being reunited after they get in other people's cars or get stolen. Without the chip, I would have spent the next few days putting up posters, asking neighbours to check their sheds, and then if no one had found her, in the weeks and months to come, maybe even for the rest of my life, I'd have imagined terrible things. That she was trapped somewhere. Lying injured but alive, in pain, crying for me. Lost and trying to find a way home. Even though I didn't have to face this scenario of not knowing, of imagining, because of the call, as I sobbed my way up and down the pool I still thought of the terrible things. I'd imagined them before so they were ready to go, like my brain had just been waiting for a chance to press play and it had chosen that day, of all days. What a traitor the brain can be.

The terrible things I'd imagined before that day, they'd never happened because she always came back. Late sometimes, so late I'd decided, *this is it, this is the day she doesn't come back.*

But then she did and it wasn't that day, it was an ordinary OK day, but better than that really because all days with her were better, the best. And now it was that day, and I did know what had happened, because of the call, because someone had seen her, hadn't turned away, had carried her, small and still, carried her to a place that was gentle with soft broken bundles at the side of the road, gentle even when there was no more pain, when all they can do is share the news. And so they scanned her for a chip, and called me, because I do what you're meant to do and keep my contact details up to date, and I was grateful — truly, though I hadn't been able to say that on the phone, because of the sobbing.

It was during length number twenty that I first heard her. The fact I could hear anything was a surprise because of my ear plugs. I thought it must be the filter or the pump — the mechanics of a swimming pool that I couldn't properly name or point out but knew must be there. Hoped were there. It was a kind of sigh. Gentle, so I knew it wasn't my sobbing, but I took my ear plugs out to be sure, and without them I couldn't hear the sound anymore and I was sobbing worse than ever, so I put my ear plugs back in and there it was again, just that sound. I felt a bit better, for the first time since the call. The sound ebbed and flowed, as if the pool was tidal. And it was a warm sound, made me feel warm. Made me feel slow, too. My arms and legs went soft and came to meet one another near my head, so I was a ball in the water, everything around me darkening. I tucked my head in, put my hands over my eyes, and listened. I knew it was her. Reaching out to me on some strange frequency. A frequency I knew existed but which was on another channel that I wasn't meant to hear yet. It was her, and

she was safe. I balled myself tighter, imagined her soft body curled into mine as if we were on the sofa. Safe.

One of the other swimmers got me out of the pool. An aquafit lady who'd stayed on for some lengths after the class. When I'd assured her, and the others blinking wetly around me, that I was all right, I found I could say the words that I hadn't been able to say when the call came. I stuck my head inside my locker and said the words. I got dressed and I got in the car and phoned them back and I said the words: thank you. I said them so many times that the car fogged up and it was like I had my tear-filled goggles on again. Thank you. Thank you. Thank you.

And then I got out of the car and went back to the changing room, put my soaked costume on again, put my salty, lash-marked goggles on too, and got back into the pool. I left my ear plugs in my locker.

It Was Nothing

by Ashley Harnett

In the dead of night, when the wind is howling, and the shadows at the end of the bed begin to look like the twisted faces of malignant foes, it can be hard to force yourself to open your eyes fully.

IT is harder still, to get out from under your safe, comfortable duvet and make your way out into the hall to investigate a sound. The sound which woke you up, the sound which you had allowed yourself to believe was the remnant of a dream but which has just repeated itself for the third time since you became conscious.

The air in your room is cold, the ageing windows do little to prevent the ingress of a breeze which has swept away the warmth of the day, this is a temperature, a time of the day, which you did not expect to experience. It is uncomfortable.

You draw in a deep breath, perhaps to steel yourself against the cold or perhaps in preparation for a sudden fearful exhalation later. You reach out and switch on the bedside lamp; it does not immediately reveal a terrifying presence in the room. You slide your legs off the edge of the bed and place your feet on the cold floor; nothing grabs your ankles from beneath the bed. You get up and walk to your door, collecting your phone as you do, grasping it tightly in your hand. You open the door but there is nothing there.

You are almost annoyed that nothing is there, nothing has frightened you. You turn away from the door and just as you close it you feel the pressure of breath on the back of your neck, cold breath, colder and more solid than the air around you in the room. You turn again but you see nothing. The fear has returned, as you hurry back to the safety of your bed you tell yourself that you'll be able to calm down and get back to sleep in a moment.

It is a while before you build up the courage to reach over and switch off the light. You drift back to sleep and, in time, the gentle light of morning washes away whatever frights you had in the night.

Hours pass before anything reminds you of your nocturnal experience. The reminder comes when you are making a late-morning cup of tea and once again the tiny hairs on the back of your neck are brought to alert by the sensation of breath.

In the comfortable safety of daylight you are emboldened, you turn immediately to confront this — well, you don't know what, you have turned to see that you are alone. The kitchen is empty, clear of intruders, the windows are closed, nothing disturbs the still calm of the room. This place is the model of comfort and safety, you think to yourself.

You turn back to your tea. It is not where you left it, just between you and the kettle. It now sits an arm's length away to your left. Did you do that? Were you holding it when you turned around?

You shrug, it's nothing, it's just a silly thought. You tell yourself that you're just feeling the loneliness of being here by yourself while your flatmate is away.

Soon your flatmate returns and nothing happens for a week or two; you're almost embarrassed to tell the story of how silly you'd been. You're no longer alone in the flat but you still spend plenty of time by yourself. Now, though, the evenings pass more quickly and if you hear a bump in the night it is easily attributed to your flatmate.

One morning, your flatmate comes to you to complain, what were you up to last night making all that banging noise? Why were you being so noisy in the middle of the night? Nothing, you insist, you were early to bed last night and nothing woke you.

Together you remember the earlier silliness, to diffuse the tension of a misdirected complaint you joke that you have a ghost in the house after all. You joke but you're thinking about all the stories you've read, all the films you've seen and you wonder to yourself what will come next. Later you read-up on 'real' ghost stories.

Doing your research has hardly helped, you're working yourself into a bit of a fuss over this. Nothing unusual is happening, you tell yourself, just the typical sounds of a quirky old building.

Days continue to pass with nothing strange going on and you decide to put it out of your mind. You feel silly again, evidently there was nothing. You feel all the sillier scaring yourself. Your flatmate has said nothing else about it. There is nothing, nothing at all to be frightened of here.

You're having a quiet night with your flatmate, a little later on, when the doorbell goes. The neighbour is asking if you're the one who's been making all the banging noises. No, you tell them, you've heard no such noises this evening let alone made them. Perhaps an animal has gotten into the attic, they suppose. Perhaps, you agree. The landlord is called; they reluctantly agree to come out and investigate the next day. Everyone seems to agree that's what it must be. Your flatmate tells you they'd actually been a bit scared when they heard the banging before and it hadn't been you — an animal in the attic never occurred to them.

The theory seems to satisfy your flatmate but it doesn't add up for you, animals in the attic can't breathe on your neck and move your tea.

You don't sleep well that night, you can't stop turning those little thoughts over in your head. When the landlord comes they find nothing in the attic, no sign of any animal or any way one might be getting in. The neighbour thinks they're just trying to avoid the issue but it seems to satisfy everyone nonetheless. It was an animal, it is gone now. You aren't convinced.

The next time you feel cold air on your neck or hear a bump in the night you will tell yourself it was nothing but the truth is you are convinced now that you have a ghost and it is floating right behind you.

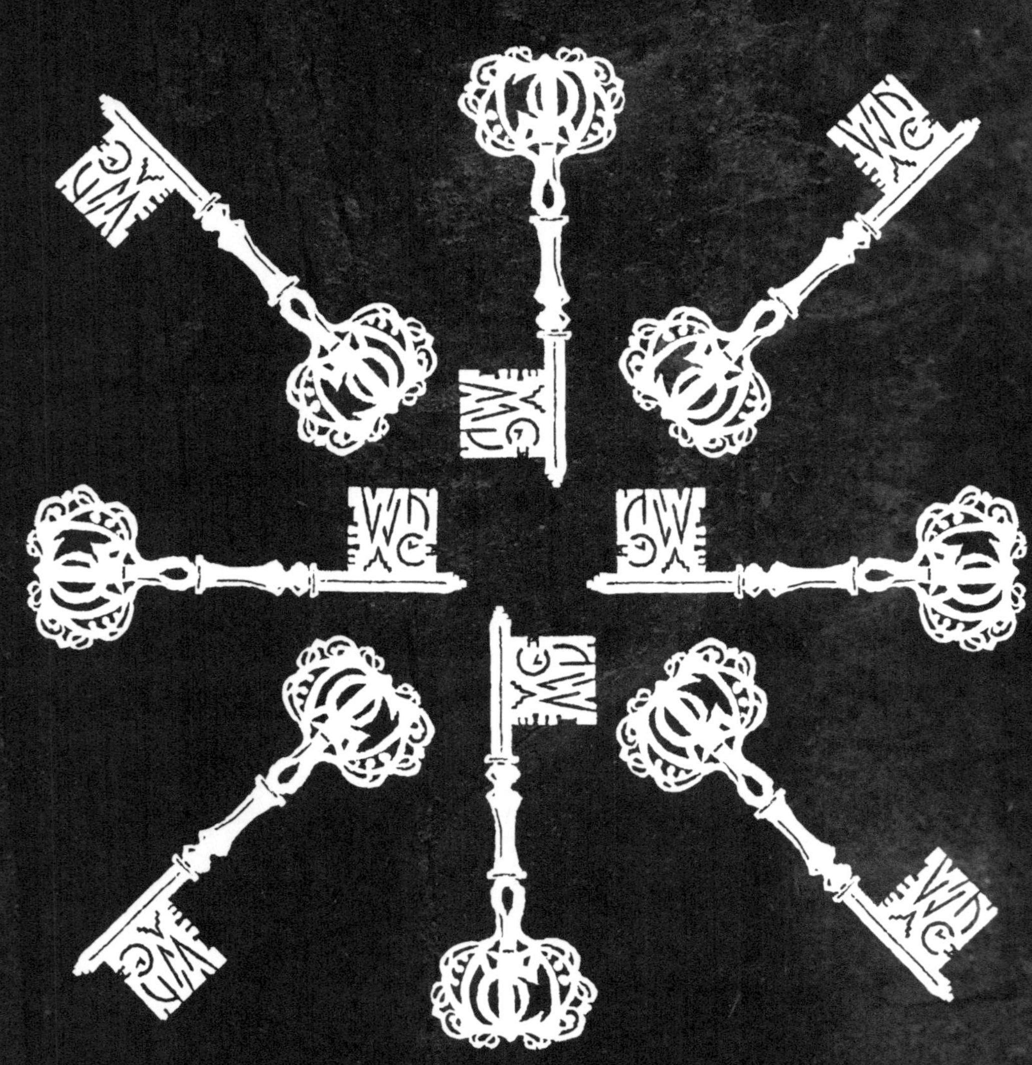

The Viewing

by Alex Gillinder

The incident? Selena asked. 'Didn't they tell you?' the small woman mumbled in her soft, low voice, as they reached the top of the stairs.

HER bare feet creaked on the old boards, sending a small cloud of dust from beneath the floor which dispersed across the landing. She'd slid out of her shoes earlier, so she could dance on her tiptoes in the dining room, humming a quiet song to herself, and had left the small black pumps down there.

Selena was uncomfortable with the letting agent's behaviour, but felt she didn't really have any case to protest. 114 Barker Lane was not her house. She had signed no documents, nor exchanged so much as a penny, and she didn't really want to upset the person who would negotiate such things. And even then, she would only be a lodger. Reaching the latter half of her thirties, Selena lamented the unlikely chances of her ever owning her own residence. The woman — Selena realised she hadn't even asked her name, and felt it was too awkward to bring it up now — had stopped. The back of her head faced Selena, waiting. Remembering the question, Selena cleared her throat a little.

'Briefly. The man on the phone — John?'

'John?' the woman repeated, and Selena thought she heard a small giggle.

'Yes, I think it was John…' No reply. 'He said there was an accident a few years ago — a girl.'

'A girl…'

Selena had been told when she'd rang up about the listing that the agency legally had to disclose that the previous tenant had been found dead in the bathroom.

'That's what I was told,' Selena replied. She was a prescriber of the sound logic that someone has likely died in every building, and knowing the ins-and-outs of those deaths would only make any move more stressful and uncomfortable. And for the price they were offering, she was more than willing to give the place a look. She found the best solution for any new move was the same as when you enter a hotel room — pretend there never was a previous occupant. Despite asking the agency not to tell her the details, they had pushed on regardless.

The official ruling was that the previous tenant had slipped whilst running a bath, and hit her head on the sink. A welfare check had been called, as the girl's brother had been unable to reach her regarding a trip they were planning, and the bath had still been running when an officer had kicked down the door some three hours later.

The small woman turned her head slightly as they entered the upstairs bathroom, so as to direct her words over her shoulder without really looking at her companion. Selena was suddenly struck by the woman's face, lit by the grey sky coming in through the frosted glass of the bathroom window. Pale, and slightly sunken, she could have only been in her thirties herself — but she had the presence of someone far older than that. Selena only now noticed that the woman's dusty blonde hair, in its loose and messy bun, had a cobweb in it.

'The knot wasn't tied properly, and it took forever…'

With that, she pulled on the string cord by the door. The bathroom light bulb flickered as it came on, and for the briefest moment in one of those flickers, Selena saw a shape thrown in shadow against the damp-speckled wall. A body, hanging, with legs kicking and flailing. Then the light was on, and showed nothing but the shadow of the light cord itself, swinging with the residual momentum left by the small woman's hand. Selena frowned at her guide.

'I'm sorry?'

'You've got to get the knot right,' came the reply, 'or the neck won't —' and with that, the pale woman made a cracking sound with her mouth.

'I thought she hit her head?' Selena was confused. The woman turned now to face her.

'Who's that, love?' she asked, and Selena couldn't help her tone as her incredulity rose in her voice.

'The tenant who *died*? The one we've been talking about?' The woman smiled, her eyes glazing over, as though lost in a long-forgotten memory of childhood.

'I get lost, sometimes. There are so many.' A pause, a lip-curl, and then a murmur. 'They hang witches in these parts, didn't you know?' she said, and before Selena could enquire further, the woman gestured to the bathroom. 'As required, toilet, sink, etcetera.' And with that, she walked past Selena and out into the passage.

The next stop was the smaller of the two bedrooms — the room Selena had earmarked for an office space to work on her writing when she had looked at the original listing. It was pretty standard — small, with room enough for a pull-out bed and maybe a small desk or one of those cheap canvas zip-up wardrobes. There was nothing particularly wrong with the room, besides the need for dusting and a good vacuum, but something wasn't quite working for her. There was a sense of something, a smudge of grey. Only when she looked around did Selena realise it was in the corner of her vision, no matter where she turned. She rubbed her eye, but it stayed there for a full minute, only fading once she had left for the main bedroom.

'I meant to ask, where is the stopcock? Last flat I rented, the toilet burst and it took us forever to find the bloody —' She stopped as she entered the room, and saw the small woman lying on the bed. Her arms were by her side, and she was staring up at the ceiling. Selena cleared her throat. 'Are... are you okay?' she asked. The woman didn't reply at first. Only when asked again did she get a response.

'You can't hear the train, can you?'

'I'm sorry?'

The woman gestured with her marble hand.

'The station is only a few minutes walk from here. Other places, even next door, they'd hear it. A train's just passed now, in fact. Screeching and clattering its way to Scotland. The platform is busy too, this time of day. But we don't hear it in here.'

'There's a cat,' Selena said, caught off-guard by both the woman's words and the creature that had just poked its head around the curtain.

A great fluffy, white creature; it sat on the windowsill, staring at her with large, unblinking eyes. 'Does that come with the house?' Selena joked, more for something to say than anything else. She'd started feeling the impatience, the need to leave.

'The cat isn't yours,' the woman said.

That was enough.

'I'm sorry, but is there anything else to see?' she asked. 'Only I have a work thing in half an hour.' A lie.

'Why did you pick this house?' the woman asked. Selena stood for a moment, unsure how to answer. She decided on the truth.

'It's cheap,' she said, 'and the photos looked good. The only viewing I've been to so far that

wasn't a manky flat. If I'm honest, I wondered why no one else had jumped on this place.' She waited for a response, as she stood swaying in the bedroom doorway. The woman turned her head.

'Some people flee from what they can't understand,' she whispered. She stretched her legs out, flexing her long toes. 'I had a brother. A kind boy, but dim. He had these dreams. Peculiar dreams you'd never believe if they hadn't come from his honest lips.'

Selena pretended to check the watch on her wrist.

'I've really got to be going —'

'He told me something, once,' came the interruption. 'After one of those dreams. He said, 'This house... it has *hands*. They are greedy hands, and once they have you...' Her voice trailed off, and a tear fell down her pale cheek and spread across the pillow beneath her head. Selena didn't understand. She knew she should just turn around and leave; abandon this place in the background of her mind, but she couldn't help it. Against her better judgement, the woman's mumblings were drawing her closer.

'Wait, you lived here? With your brother?' she asked, and saw a small crease in her companion's brow.

'Lived here?' The answer was slow, forced, as though she was only half-listening, or sedated. It seemed like an age until she finished her answer. 'I suppose we've all lived here, at one point or another. Don't you agree?'

It was raining when Selena left the front door of 114 Barker Lane and half-ran to her car. Through the downpour, she felt something, like when a small child pulls on their parent's coat for attention. She did not look back. Instead, before she pulled away, she called another agency and accepted the conditions for one of the flats she'd seen a few days before.

A week or so later, Selina's colleague was talking about their search for a place with their partner. They showed her a few screenshots of listings on their phone, and one of them was Barker Lane. Selena wanted to say something, warn her friend of the strange woman who had shown her around, but couldn't bring herself to. With the space between then and now, she'd written off the viewing as one of those strange things in life it's best to ignore. When they mentioned that they'd been told by the agent that a man who'd lived there had thrown himself down the stairs, they asked if it was morbid to view the place. Selena gave a polite shrug, and pretended to be invested in her work until someone else answered.

The colleague moved in shortly afterwards. Selena feigned a reason not to go to the housewarming, and spent that whole night staring at the dead static on her television and ignoring the gentle tug that kept pulling at her ponytail.

Just before Christmas that year, Craig, the manager, came into the office with a sombre look on his face. Even before he spoke, Selena knew her friend was dead.

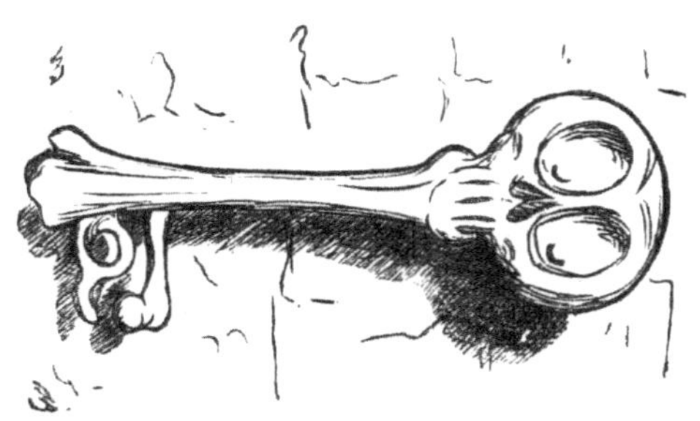

These gloomy stairs, so dark,
so damp, so cold.

Pullus galli
naceus mon-
strosus.

Peregrination

by Simon John Parkin

Illustration by Hannah Durham

G OD, I hate pigeons, with their oil-slick necks and warted beaks. Their feathers seem to clog my throat even when they're sitting on the other side of strengthened glass, like this one is now, balled up in a bed of its own feathery shit. It hops out of the brown-spattered nest it's made in the corner of my window ledge and hobbles up and down on a deformed foot that looks like chewed-up gum.

How grey pigeons are; how perfectly suited to the clouds that hang over this godforsaken hill; how dull and conventional like the fogies that throng Dudley Market in their colourless, double-breasted Mackintoshes, pecking at cut-price meat squirming in plastic bags or cooing about the fence that the neighbours have erected in front of their rhododendrons.

Who cares if pigeons can find their way home using some weird in-built navigation system as if a compass has been stapled onto their maggot-brains? What's so good about home when it's halfway up a pebble-dashed tower block in the West Midlands?

I wouldn't stay here if I had wings. Or if my leg wasn't withered inside its cast like a spat-out dog chew. Falls outside pubs didn't bother me when I was young but now my limbs snap like cheap plastic at the slightest tumble, trip or shove. Tutting paramedics scrape my remains off the pavement and tuck my broken glasses into my top pocket before carting me away. Metal rods are inserted into what's left of my crumbling bones. I get dumped back in my flat to fester in a wheelchair, dosed up on codeine, watching black and white war movies until I fall asleep — bottle in hand — to the drones of incoming Messerschmitts, waking up wet to the distorted thud of machine guns. Fresh-faced nurses check up on me once a week, try to change my piss-stained pyjamas, restock my painkillers and scold me for not doing my exercises. They look shocked when I lash out at them with a well-placed fist, or tell them where to stick their sodding exercises.

The pigeon glares at me from behind the glass with one bulbous red eye, stabbing its podgy head in front of it while emitting a continuous, 'Who? Who? Who?' from somewhere inside its germ-ridden body.

'What?' I shout. 'What the bloody hell do you want?!'

I rap my metal walking stick against the glass making the pigeon clatter up into the air. It circles between the three tower blocks, flying up then gliding down, round and round beneath the carpet of clouds like a thing possessed, waiting to darken my window ledge once more as if none of the other fifty or so ledges will do.

Then, for just a moment, the clouds part and a ray of sunlight escapes. A shape like the falling head of an axe crashes down onto the pigeon making it drop out of the sky in a flailing ball of blood and feathers.

The sight makes me gasp.

I'd read an article in the *Express & Star* about a local nesting peregrine but hadn't actually seen it until now. It gracefully loops around and dives after the falling bird, catching it with muscly legs. The pigeon's broken neck dangles beneath the falcon's speckled undercarriage.

The peregrine lands on top of the tower block opposite and hunches over its kill, glaring around, jealously guarding the dead pigeon, clutching its body with bright yellow talons. It plucks a few feathers from the pigeon's chest with a great hook of a beak then punctures its skin, prises the body apart and digs its head in, tugging out sinews, gulping them down until its creamy bib turns red.

I have never seen anything so swift yet majestic, so brutal yet impassive. The way the pigeon's pathetic life is snuffed out so instantly and without remorse makes me tremble as I imagine the god-like power of this awesome bird of prey. For a few moments, I'm no longer bound to this dismal flat with constant pain from my leg. I'm flying, slicing the air at a hundred miles an hour. Raining death and destruction on those beneath me. King of this hill. Lord of the skies. Free to soar.

Over the next few days, I don't watch telly anymore; I have my very own dogfight to watch outside the window as the peregrine terrorises the local pigeon population, diving out of the sky as if from the sun itself, corralling its prey using the three tower blocks as bluffs, plucking birds from the air as casually as picking berries from a bush. My failing eyes can just about see it devouring its catch on the tower block opposite but I need to get closer; I want to see those disgusting pigeons get their hearts ripped through their filthy chest cavities.

I drop a few pieces of raw chicken breast on my window ledge to try and lure the peregrine closer. Its scowling eyes look at the morsel with disdain as it swoops past. Why scavenge the cold scraps of a caged mutant when warm pigeon blood is on the menu? I try throwing it crumbled sausage, strands of mince from a tin, even a bit of tuna, but all I get at my window are more pigeons who squabble over the meat until it falls into the courtyard below.

I sit at the window and watch the peregrine's daily acrobatic display, its swooping and soaring, its effortless gliding as if gravity were a concern for lesser mortals. As I slowly drain my bottle of vodka, a long-lost memory from school surfaces: a rare moment of joy when my glasses weren't being stamped on or when I wasn't being hauled to the headmistress's office to have another talk about 'personal hygiene'. It reminds me of when the animal man visited.

Out of the various sorry-looking creatures that the animal man pulled from the back of his caged van, I didn't care about the gormless rabbits that sat on our crossed legs like fat balls of fluff and I wasn't bothered about stroking the catatonic reptiles; the only beast I was enraptured with was the barn owl. After showing us its semi-revolving head and asymmetric ears, the man placed the owl on a perch at the back of the hall. He walked to the stage — the owl watching him the whole time — put on a huge leather glove and whirled a piece of meat around on the end of a piece of string.

I remember the whoosh, the breeze that ruffled my hair as the huge bird silently whipped across the hall, inches above our heads, to snatch the swinging morsel from the air followed by a chorus of 'ooh's.

It gives me an idea.

I wheel myself over to the kitchen and rummage through a drawer until I find some old fishing line. I tie up a piece of chicken breast and hang it from the end of my walking stick. I push it out the window so that the meat swings back and forth in the wind then wedge the stick in the window frame.

It only takes an hour or so for the peregrine to spot the suspended meat and attempt a couple of fly-bys.

Then, it happens so quickly I almost miss it: rolling so that its wings are parallel to the tower block wall, claws first, as fast as a slap across the face, it snatches the whirling piece of meat from the end of the line.

For the first time in weeks, through the pain that radiates up my broken leg, I smile. I almost laugh. Now, I can see the peregrine in all its glory: its huge merciless eyes that locate the bait so accurately, its perfectly streamlined body that storms past my window, the vice-like claws that catch the meat right before my eyes.

What I wouldn't give to be as agile and unfettered, as liberated as that bird.

I repeat my baiting the next day with matched success and again the day after. The peregrine seems to become more confident with my offerings, like I'm gaining its trust. Over the weeks, it strikes more gracefully, more acrobatically, showing off its skills as if thanking me for the food, and I feel utterly thrilled each time it does.

Two burly paramedics throw me into the back of an ambulance like they're sending me to the knacker's yard. My kicks and screams are met with indifference. I wait all day in bleached corridors for a man to hack my cast off with an electric saw, exposing the flaccid yellow skin on

a leg I don't recognise. The doctor grimaces when he bandages it. He tells me to use it more, to not be so lazy. I give him the finger. When the paramedics slam my flat door behind them that evening, I hear one hope that the 'fat, four-eyed waste of space will be dead of liver failure soon'.

I haul myself out of the wheelchair and into bed and sip from a bottle of vodka until the smell of hospital finally leaves me.

The nagging, biting pain in my leg wakes me around noon the next day. After washing a couple of codeine down, I put my glasses on and wheel myself into the dark living room. Putting my weight on one foot, the bandaged leg left hanging limp, I reach up to the curtains. When I whip them open, a bloody face stares at me making me fall back into my chair.

The peregrine sits on the window ledge, speckled chest puffed out, brown plumage ruffling in the wind and a half-dead pigeon spasming in its beak. It pecks at the window, shaking the pigeon as it does, striking the glass so hard I think it might shatter. A cloud of grey feathers blows away as the helpless pigeon tries to escape, thrashing to no avail.

'What?' I shout, my voice cracking, but, somehow, I know what it wants. Trembling, my actions not quite my own, I slide the window down.

The peregrine hops up onto the open window and perches there, outstretched wings blocking the light. Without breaking its stare, it ragdolls the pigeon, snapping its neck, then drops the limp body onto my lap with a wet thud.

An eye drapes from the pigeon's head and dark blood oozes out of its punctured throat.

I scream and push the bird off, kicking my wheelchair backwards, away from the window and the peregrine, knocking the telly off its stand in my panic.

The peregrine takes one more look at me, turns, then launches itself from my window onto the updraught of the tower block before disappearing into the clouds.

Still shaking, I kick the remains of the pigeon out of my flat door and into the corridor, leaving a red smear across the lino.

I keep my window and curtains shut for the rest of the day.

That night, I crack the top off a bottle of vodka and guzzle it down. I squirm around in bed, desperately trying to shake the thought of that hideous silhouette in my window, the warm carcass in my lap, the pigeon's eyeball creeping along my thigh, until I fall into a restless sleep.

A great storm cloud rises over the hill. I try to run for cover, but I can't. One of my ankles is caught in a snare that bites to the bone. I look up and I'm in my flat and the cloud is blowing through my letterbox. No, it's not... it's a person: a woman in a brown Mackintosh. My bedroom door explodes from its hinges as she bounds in and leaps onto the bed. A horrific screech emanates from her hooked nose. I cry out, but she puts a feathery hand over my face and holds me down. I kick and punch until I wake up, drenched in sweat.

At first, I think I punched one of my pillows apart in my sleep because I am surrounded by feathers. They cover my bedclothes and chest and stick to my face where I've been lying on them.

I look again and notice that they have a grey, oily sheen.

I retch and spit, coughing the pigeon feathers from my tongue and pulling them from between my teeth.

Something stops me. This doesn't seem right. I feel like I'm being watched.

There, at the end of my bed, perched on the footboard, enormous black eyes glistening in the dark, blood dripping from its beak, sits the peregrine.

It slowly stretches its wings so that they fill the room.

It lets out a high, piercing screech that rises like a siren.

It leans towards me, looms right over me, then takes flight.

Dark wings envelop me. Talons clutch my throat and rip it open, instantly silencing my gargled scream. The blood runs down my neck and pools onto the mattress. I try to swallow but feel the peregrine's beak burrowing down into my throat, pulling at the arteries and tendons. Its whole head is in my chest now, covered in blood and going deeper, down into my stomach, pecking and yanking, devouring lungs and kidneys

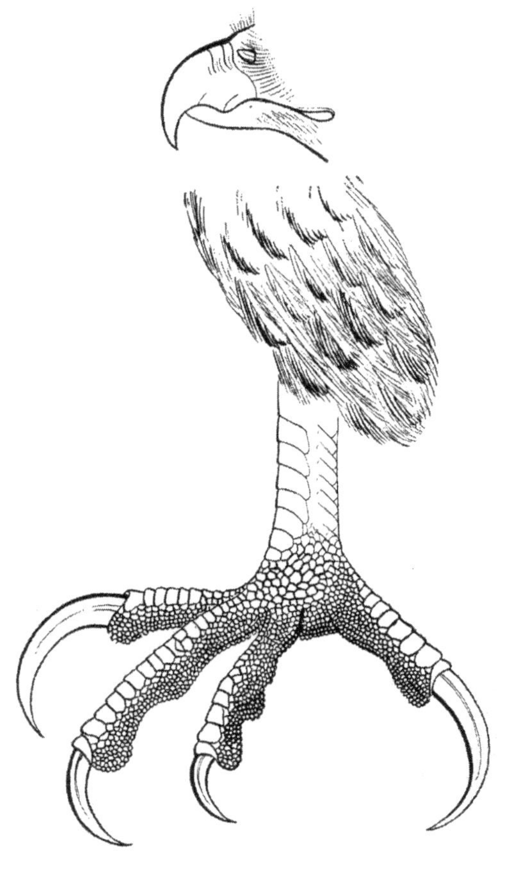

and intestines until there's nothing left but his flapping, frenzied body.

I jolt awake and immediately vomit over my bedclothes.

I sit there, trying to catch my breath, an acrid taste in my mouth.

As I push my soiled bed clothes aside, something fist-sized drops to the floor from the pool of my vomit. I poke the grey object with an outstretched finger and it rolls, rounded and hairy, like a limbless, beheaded rat. Except it's not hair; it's feathers, tightly bound in a ball of dried mucus. I kick it under the wardrobe in disgust and it leaves behind the small white bone of a bird.

Tentatively, I open the living room curtains, dreading the sight of that peregrine coming back to taunt me, but it's not there. I quickly scan the sky. Everything seems ill-defined and grainy so I take my glasses off to wipe them. Before I can put them back on I notice that the view from my window suddenly appears in technicolour. Every window on the tower block opposite glows with detail: the pattern on each set of curtains is crisp, every thread of polyester shivers like water. I instantly count nine pigeons, three young and feeble, teetering on the edge of their shit-spattered nests, but no peregrine.

Thank god for that, I think, and put my glasses in my top pocket.

I wheel myself to the kitchen in search of breakfast. The smell of sour milk and weeks-old margarine rises from the fridge when I open it. I take out the last piece of chicken I was saving for the peregrine and breathe in the sharp, tangy aroma. Suddenly, the raw slab of meat is in my mouth and I'm tearing at it, pulling it apart with clenched teeth, thrashing my head from side to side, gulping it down, blood dribbling down my chin. As the last piece of chicken slides down my throat I look around to check that nobody saw me.

If anything, the food makes me even more hungry. I have to get some meat from the market, even though the thought of mixing with those fogies makes me queasy.

In the bedroom, I pull clothes from piles scattered around the room. As I tug a sock over my foot, I rip a ladder into the brown nylon with my long and curled toenails. I put an old pair of trainers on my bare feet instead.

Once I'm dressed, I stand up to put my overcoat on. I look down in disbelief. The pain in my leg: it's gone! Not just eased off like when I've necked a few codeine, but completely gone as if the last few weeks were a nightmare I've just

woken up from. I test my foot by stamping it on the lino. It feels strong, the muscles powerful.

This will show that stupid doctor who's lazy, I think.

In the lift, my hand hovers over the ground floor button. I press number 19 instead: the top floor. Maybe some fresh air will quell this insatiable hunger.

On the roof, the air fills my lungs like a balloon. The confinement, the pain and the humiliation of being cooped up for so long, drift from my body like a shower of feathers.

I walk to the edge of the roof, fearless for once. The updraught blows my brown overcoat open, making it ruffle and flap.

I stretch my arms as wide as they will go and take in the view. The vast conurbation of the West Midlands stretches to the Shropshire hills on the horizon and the streets between my feet pulse with people like blood along arteries.

Everything is clear to me now.

The bodies that waddle along like useless bags of meat are identical. Purposeless and insignificant, they scratch out a living, surviving on scraps, thankful for the respite of their shitty houses at the end of each miserable day.

I could swoop down and pluck their boring grey brains out.

They are beneath me now.

Never again will I endure their snide comments, their disapproving looks.

No judgements or insults or sly feet extended from underneath tables can darken my days any more.

I will not be caged.

I am different.

Better.

Best.

A gap appears in the clouds and a ray of sunshine breaks free as I step off the building.

Finally, I can soar, lord of the skies, king of the hill.

I slice through the air at a hundred miles an hour. Two hundred. Rocketing down.

Graceful at last.

And I'm no longer bound to this grey, godforsaken land.

ROMA
Via del Mare - Rupe Tarpea.
Rue de la Mer - Roche Tarpénene.
Via del Mare - Tarpejan Rock.
Via del Mare - tarpejischen Felsn.
PRESTITO
REND
1935 - "Fotografinide,, Cesare Capello-Milano

Nancy

by Mat Troy

Nick risked a quick sideways glance at the young woman in the fifties style skirt, raincoat and plastic bonnet beside him in the car.

HER gloved hands tightened around the reassuring thick brown leather strap of her slightly scuffed handbag and he marvelled at how real she looked. The story shouldn't open on the ghost, he felt it should build to that, but there she was.

The misty rain ahead of them swirled in symmetrical formations, illuminated in the headlights of the small car as it cut cautiously through the night, like an icebreaker navigating an ominous polar sea.

'You've got a really nice car,' she said softly, over the rhythmic, reassuring squeak-thud of his wipers. The surprise of anyone thinking his musty smelling, nineteen year old Toyota was impressive scored nearly as high as the sentence being said by a real ghost. 'Your dashboard reminds me of the jukebox at Alfred's.'

'Alfred's Cafe in Lewiston?' He replied, risking another glance at her moon pale but remarkably solid face besides him, wishing immediately that he hadn't sounded so condescending. 'Didn't they close down?'

'Don't be daft,' replied Nancy. The ghost was called Nancy. 'I was there on Wednesday!' She shifted in her seat huffing defensively, but something in her voice said she was suddenly not a hundred percent certain of that fact.

Nick didn't blame her, his car wouldn't have looked like any she'd been in before. His demeanour was probably weird, he had no idea how Fifties men spoke to Fifties women and if it was any different to how he might speak to women now. It wasn't as if he was an expert in that particular field anyway.

'My mistake.' He scrambled to roll back his poorly judged words, conscious of upsetting her again. The dashboard she'd mentioned was twenty years old to him, but fifty years in the future for her, the perfectly ordinary LED displays probably looked very unusual and space aged, or not, technically she was the one from the space age, not him.

He caught her pulling the handbag closer and shifting again in her seat. Ghost or not, she was still a woman in a car with a strange man who had picked her up from that isolated bend on a rainy December's night on the Welsh borders. This ghost was more scared of him than he was of her and she didn't even seem to remember that she'd been in his car before.

The first time Nick had seen Nancy, she'd unsurprisingly terrified him. He'd been driving home late from a server installation at his company's new office near Shrewsbury. Despite being the most reliable tech in his business he had the navigational skills of a hot air balloon, so had predictably got lost on his way home to Mid Wales and had ended up on the back roads.

As the occasional houses turned into farm tracks, he was fully aware of the reputation of these corners and very much did not want to be stuck in a ditch where the phone signal was as mythical as the forest around him. He'd turned the radio off to help him think, so only had the hum of his engine and the percussion of his wipers as he'd taken the bend and as she came into view he'd felt his heart jump to his throat.

His first impression was this was one of those schemes you heard about on YouTube, where you stop for someone and they box your car in, kidnap you, and steal your kidneys. When he got close and saw a sad looking woman in a long green winter coat, hand on the back of her head as if to stop her vintage rain bonnet being blown away by the wind, his good conscience got the better of him and he pulled over. He told her he was headed in the direction of the town of Llanidloes and she nodded and got in. He was then horrified a second time, when after a minute or two of awkward small talk, she'd vanished into thin air without opening the door.

Nick had obsessed over the experience for days. He tried blaming long work hours, the recent change in his meds and being on his own for too long. He'd messaged the other techs on his team to ask them if they believed in ghosts but the response had been to make fun of him for being credulous. He'd decided not to tell them anything else. Nick wasn't exactly a gregarious person and found it easier just to internalise these things, go back to communicating in memes and *Family Guy* gifs and forget the whole thing.

Except, he couldn't get this Green Lady out of his head, and the following Friday had found himself driving down that creepy forest route in the opposite direction. That second time he'd seen Nancy he had lost his nerve and sped on, not stopping until he found himself at some small town on the English side of the border where he could get a coffee from the local garage and sit somewhere surrounded by lights and concrete.

Not entirely sure why he was doing it, he'd found himself making the journey the next night and this time had mustered the courage to stop, trembling in terror as she approached the vehicle. She'd got into his car and he'd tried to gently explain to her she was a ghost. This had not gone well and had upset her before she disappeared again.

For a few days after this she was a no show and Nick was worried he'd lost her. Then on Saturday evening, he was on his seventh trip through the woods when he spotted her on her regular bend. She didn't seem to remember him and he conducted a journey of almost half a mile with her before she faded away for reasons he couldn't quite understand.

After another two trips he'd managed to get her name and then a little more of her story. She'd been left by the roadside by someone after an argument. It hadn't made sense, being left by the roadside didn't seem enough to make a ghost of a person. The bend was only about a mile from the nearest farm house in either direction and as creepy a journey that would have been at night, even in winter, it shouldn't have been lethal. He'd considered that if it had been snowing then maybe, but nothing about her outfit suggested it was anything more than maybe a grey and dreary day when she set out.

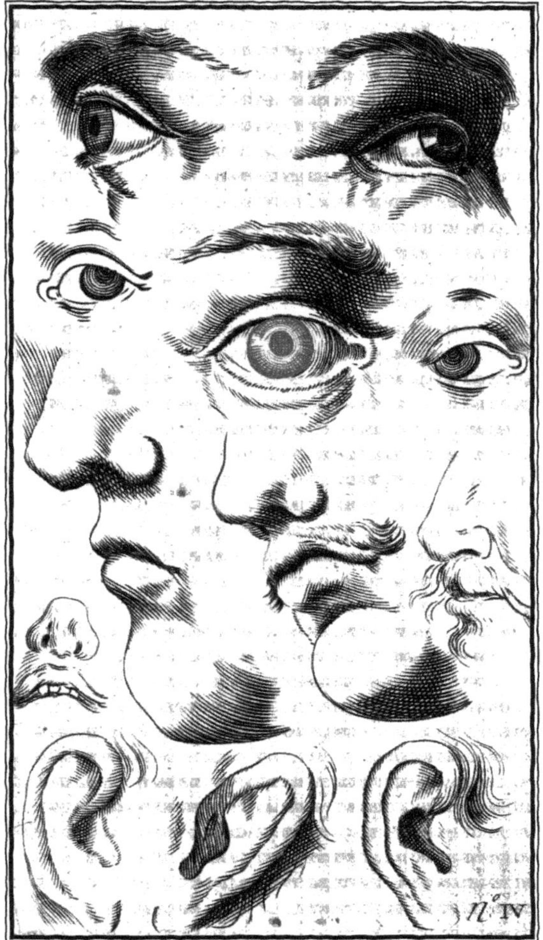

There'd been a moment's silence between them since he'd accidentally mentioned Alfred's cafe. Outside, their entire reality appeared to be made up of fat raindrops and the road ahead that the car swallowed as quickly as his lights could create. A quiet stretch in the pitch black of a Welsh winter. He leaned over and turned the heater up to counteract the cold from outside, or maybe from her, he'd read that ghosts in classic hauntings sometimes made things cold.

The silence had lasted so long that Nick was half expecting to look over and see she'd disappeared, but when he chanced a look at her he found she was crying instead.

'Nancy, are you ok?' he asked tentatively.

'Oh… Oh no,' she said quietly, sniffing and dabbing her eyes.

'What?' Nick felt a rising sense of unease, he was not good with this sort of thing. His eyes darted between her and the road as he eased off the accelerator to give himself more reaction time in an emergency.

'Well, I never told you my name, did I?' She said, looking straight ahead as if to conceal her expression.

'Not tonight, no.' Nick considered trying to explain himself further but from past experience brevity seemed the wiser option.

'It's strange,' she said softly. 'The longer I'm here the more I know I've been here before, and the harder it is to stay here.'

'Nancy, I…' he began.

'Nick.' She took a breath, or at least went through the bodily motions of taking a breath. 'Am I dead?'

'I'm so sorry.'

'No.' she said in a wretched whimper.

'It's ok, it's ok.' He tried to reassure her, knowing that it very much was not, feeling more out of his depth in a social situation than he ever had in a life that had been nothing but awkward interactions.

'It's not though, is it? I'm bloody dead, love!' She started a bitter laugh which collapsed into a fraught sob. 'Pull over.' She said, her voice breaking, 'I have the worst luck with fellers on this road.'

Starting to feel a rising dread inside him, Nick pulled the car into a layby. The wheels crushed the wet gravel over the tick-tocking of the indicator as he slowed to a halt, the car falling silent and allowing the patter of raindrops to continue as a solo. The car lights imposed temporary daylight on a thicket of hawthorn and offended a barn owl that took off silently, momentarily distracting them.

'It's happened before.' He responded more as a statement than a question.

'You don't end up dead on the side of a road at my age without a little help, love.' Nancy nodded. 'Let me show you something.' She raised her gloved fingers to her chin and slowly undid the string on her rain bonnet with a crinkle of plastic.

Nick's stomach sank as she turned for him to inspect the back of her head. A single long slightly curved dent caved in at a slight angle from one side to the other, centering on the base of her skull, the whole area was covered in thick dark red blood flecked with dirt and detritus from the forest floor.

'Strange lonely men,' she sighed before taking his hand in hers, for a moment she held it there and then quietly whispered, 'Oh God.' Her touch felt like TV static or pins and needles. She ran her hand over his, and then squeezed it briefly, intensifying the strange tingling feeling then let him go. Her chest rose and fell beneath her coat in her ghostly simulacrum of breathing. Her eyes searched his, 'how many years?'

'Maybe seventy.' Nick replied apologetically.

She closed her eyes, collecting herself as Nick's hand slowly recovered from the bizarre sensation. A frown furrowed Nancy's brow, her eyes opened filled with something else, another emotion he wasn't sure he could recognise.

'Sorry I had to show you that.' She lifted her sticky looking rain bonnet from her lap and placed it neatly back on her head and before he could open his mouth she'd vanished.

Nancy looked different tonight. With no basis for comparison, the last few times he'd picked her up, he'd just assumed she'd looked as real as he did. This time, she seemed more real and at the same time somehow less human. It felt to Nick like seeing the latest generation of graphics for a video game, or a remaster of an old TV show. She had pulled down the sun shade to look at the tiny mirror, her face looked haggard, dark under the eyes, dirt on her coat and under her fingernails, her makeup slightly smudged.

'...I'm sorry,' said Nick, 'I wasn't really sure what to do. I thought it might be best to come back and ask.'

Their journey across this corporeal and the uncanny valley was paused briefly now while he learned what to do. They were parked at the roadside again, the hills and the forest around them felt especially pervasive tonight. His little car had stopped feeling like his pocket of civilization carving through these wild lands. It seemed as if anything might feasibly emerge from the woods tonight. Nick momentarily entertained the notion that Nancy herself might be a lure for something worse, like something from the urban legends and creepypastas that rushed through his mind. He quickly put the idea out of his head, partly for respect and partly because his mind could only barely conceive what was happening in front of him without considering other more frightening layers.

'As strange as this might seem to you.' Nancy nodded slowly, her voice came from deep within tonight, dry and hoarse like the creak of a coffin lid. 'I'm no expert on being dead, I just sort of make connections in my mind and sometimes they seem to make sense. I might even know more than I'm letting on, but as long as we're talking there's information that just doesn't flow freely.'

Nick thought about all he had read about ghosts these last few weeks. Stone tape theory, locational hauntings, poltergeists. Was it just that ghosts were trapped here in the silicates in the rock? Was that why she kept disappearing, was she losing her psychic Bluetooth signal?

'P-Perhaps I can help in some way?' he stammered.

'You've done enough,' she said, though not unkindly. She stared at something he couldn't see, like she'd pulled up screen menus in her field of vision. 'I think I was just about gone, barely even aware, then you and your bloody loneliness came around my bend and I felt it reaching out and it started feeding me.' She reached over and patted him on the knee giving him pins and needles again. 'Maybe it's time we let me fade out again, love. I think it'll take a while but a while is nothing when you've got eternity. Better things to follow, yeah?'

Nick suddenly felt the awful weight of what he had been doing here. Lying in bed the previous night he'd wondered what energies empowered her apparition. Fire needed heat, fuel and oxygen to exist, maybe his presence was completing a ghostly triad of needs. Lighting a fire in the dark and making what had been nothing but a fading shade at the roadside a solid being with presence and awareness.

'Ghost stories usually build up to the reveal.' She said pulling the car door handle and stepping out into the night 'This one ends with just you, your rocketship car, in these old woods, on your own.'

Nick opened his mouth to say something, but Nancy shook her head and he nodded silently instead.

'Good luck.' She smiled at him.

She stepped out of the vehicle and made her way in an eerily smooth motion across the wet grass at the verge of the forest, the dark stain on the back of her rain bonnet visible until she moved into the treeline. Just before she disappeared for the last time he saw something, like he had briefly caught a glimpse of the coding behind reality. He wasn't sure if that was Nancy's doing, it was a special time of year, or if he was just very open to seeing things like that right now. There were people in there, or ideas of people, passing through each other, like someone had drawn over images on a sheet of paper over and over again. There were unsettling non-human shapes there too. He wasn't sure if they were part of our reality and had too passed into another realm or they had just always existed outside our perception, working on the source code of the universe. Fortunately, none of them seemed interested in him.

The rain started to pick up again, tapping on his roof then rolling more vigorously in an impatient gust of wind that reminded him to get moving. It was indeed just him alone in his car, in this wood — ordinary Nick. He took a deep breath to help gauge how his heart felt and let it catch on a sharp snag in his chest for the loss of Nancy. Something in that made him feel more than just ordinary and that seemed enough. His foot pushed the accelerator and for the last time on that stretch his little car vanished into the galaxy of raindrops.

The Return

by Emma Oxley

*I had vowed that I would never return
to the village.*

ET there I was, just weeks after I'd made my last departure, juddering along the grassy lane toward it once again. The rickety old stagecoach that carried me creaked alarmingly with every bump and turn, as though ready to fall to pieces around me. It seemed my re-entrance was going to be as undignified as my exit before it had been.

I braced myself with one hand against the empty seat beside me as the carriage rocked from side to side, trying to prepare myself mentally for what lay ahead. Yet how could I?

The crumpled letter from Father had rolled out of my lap and onto the floor some hours before, but I hadn't bothered to retrieve it. Having read the words it contained so many times throughout the journey, I could now recite them verbatim.

My chest tightened; the inside of the carriage had begun to feel stale and airless. Reaching upward, I pulled at the laces to lower the window. As it slid down, the familiar smells of wood smoke, peat fires and manure hit my nose, the combination being symbolic of the village in which I had grown up. For better or for worse, I was home.

As I craned to look out of the opening, I noticed that Arthur, one of the market traders, was walking up the lane in our direction. Between us, we'd only ever exchanged a word or two, yet the sight of him reassured me somehow. My own grief, and the resentment I felt towards my father had driven me to leave the village after Elizabeth's funeral, not the place itself or its inhabitants. I realised how much I had missed the familiar faces and routines, every day of village life being largely the same as the day before. So different from life in the city.

Arthur moved to one side to make way for us, and I nodded a greeting as we passed him by. At first, he did not react, seeming only to look through me, before his expression hardened. He turned his face away, spitting into the dirt beside him.

My cheeks burning, I ducked my head back into the dimness of the carriage. Perhaps he had not seen me, I reasoned, but I was lying to myself. Memories of my conduct during my last visit replayed across my mind's eye, taunting me. Gossip spread like wildfire in small villages, and I had given people a lot to talk about. Still, I thought churlishly, it was hardly Arthur's place to express any judgement against me, the son of the Baron!

I dropped my head into my hands, rubbing furiously at my closed eyelids. It seemed I was not above expecting deference when it suited me. What hypocrisy I displayed!

Once I was sure we had left him behind, I turned to the open window again, willing myself to calm down before we reached our destination. Let them talk, I thought, why should I care what anyone in this godforsaken place thinks about anything? I so wished that I didn't.

The lane had smoothed out now and we were travelling through the marketplace, which was winding down for the day as the sun began to set and the shadows lengthened. A few people still milled around, and despite everything, I found myself looking for Elizabeth's face amongst them. I recalled seeing her there for the very first time, the way she had looked at me when I had introduced myself, one eyebrow arched as though not expecting very much.

I had liked that she did not defer to me like most others did. I had liked the conversations we had together. Mostly, I had just liked her.

It was clear that I had disrupted all of Father's plans for me, first with my studies that took me to the city for long periods, then by marrying without his blessing. Despite his disgruntlement, he had shown only courtesy towards Elizabeth, and she had cared for him as well as any daughter-in-law could. If only I hadn't gone away again to study, everything might have been fine. Yet how could I have known what would happen?

As we rounded a corner, a small boy ran out in front of the stagecoach. We lurched and I heard the horses braying as he ducked their flailing hooves and ran on, towards the Inn. About halfway there, he swivelled on his bare feet, his eyes meeting mine through the carriage window. They glinted in the waning sunlight, his lips curling up at the corners as he stood, staring back at me, statue still. Disturbed, I was about to look away when he suddenly turned and ran on again, through the group of men that milled outside the Inn, disappearing through the wooden door.

'You nearly had this over, then!'

A woman shouted over her shoulder as she came out, holding a jug in front of her swollen stomach. As the stagecoach clattered by, she put her hands up to her cheeks, letting go of the jug in the process. It thumped down at her feet, ale frothing out into the dirt, to loud hoots and brays from most of the patrons.

Only two of the gentlemen declined to join in, paying little heed to the carousing around them. They sat apart from the rest, playing a game of cards on top of a barrel. Their faces were familiar, as they'd occupied the space outside the Inn almost daily for as long as I could remember. I wondered how it would feel to have nothing else to do at the day's end but sit with a friend and a pack of cards in the dying sunlight. To find simple contentment in such pastimes, day after day, feeling little need for change.

How I envied them.

Son,

There is little time, and so I must write in a hurry.

Do you remember all those books you used to read? All the legends that used to fascinate you so, concerning Spirits, Black dogs, Vampires and the like? Do you recall the story about the plague villages, where the spirits of the dead were said to have risen from their graves to feed on the living, sickening them? I hope you do, even if I took those books away, not wanting your head filled with foolishness.

I was the fool, son.

We did not get much chance to speak when you were last home, and there are things I must tell you.

You will remember that when Elizabeth's friend, Martha, passed away, I wrote to you that Elizabeth had taken it as well as could be expected. At first, this was true, but soon after I sent the letter, Elizabeth claimed to have seen Martha, standing outside the kitchen window.

She had the beginnings of a fever, and I assumed her delirious, arranging for her to be cared for in her room.

As you know, the fever progressed quickly. Though I sent word to you to return from your studies as soon as I could, it was too late. You made it clear at the funeral that you cannot forgive me for that, which pains me greatly, but that is a conversation we must save for another day.

After the funeral, the gossip started. Villagers said they had seen Martha knocking on doors around the village in the middle of the night, asking to be let in. Fool that I am, I can easily dismiss the stories that are brought to my door, and I did, but I cannot so easily dismiss the object of them, when that knocks upon it.

I am sorry to have to tell you that, when Martha did come, she was not alone.

Elizabeth walks, son. I have seen her myself.

Martha has been dealt with. There is only one thing we can do for Elizabeth now. I know that you would have no one else do what must be done, and so I have ordered that her remains are to be undisturbed until you arrive. Her resting place will be guarded until then. I know that you will do your duty. For Elizabeth's sake and for the sake of the village you must, but please make haste, for if she arises the guards will act in your absence and then there will be yet another way in which I have failed you both.

Your loving father,
Edward

The words my father had written to me raced through my head as the carriage left the centre of the village and began to climb the hill. I seethed with disbelief that he would even attempt such an obscene ruse to get me to come back! It was cruel, even for him.

And yet. The village had been quieter than I had ever known for the time of day. And the strange reaction that some had shown towards my arrival had made me feel uncomfortable. As the Baron's son, I had always been treated with respect and deference, even if I had pushed against it.

What had happened here? My time in the city had certainly opened my eyes to how backwards looking a lot of places could be, but I had never seen my own village that way.

The reception I'd received, although unusual, could be explained. Many had witnessed my being escorted out of the churchyard by some of my father's men before I had left the village. My grief had been all consuming, as had my need for someone to blame. There had certainly been much gossip regarding my behaviour. Likely I had been made out to be some sort of brute.

As for the letter, it was clearly nothing more than my father trying to bring me back under his control, no matter how selfish and absurd the means.

I couldn't face the idea of going to see him just yet. There was something else I must do first. When the coachman slowed the horses in front of my family home, I told him to continue onwards, keeping my eyes fixed firmly ahead as we passed by the house.

The incline grew steeper as we headed for the Churchyard atop the hill. There was no jolting and juddering now, the lane being well worn by decades of funeral bier processions and the feet of worshippers. The air was turning cooler as the sun disappeared over the horizon and the haziness of approaching dusk fell over the hills surrounding. Shivering, I put my head down and closed my eyes, listening to the hollow clip-clopping of the horse's hooves against the ground and the squeaking surrounds of the carriage I occupied.

Shortly, we slowed and came to a stop. I looked up, expecting to see the gates of the churchyard just ahead, but they were still some distance up the hill. I heard the coachman cursing from his box and the cracking of a whip. The horses snorted, yet still we did not progress any further.

'What's the matter?' I called.

'I don't know, sir.' The coachman answered, clearly disgruntled, climbing down to stand alongside the carriage. 'Could be that one of the wheels has caught on something. I'll take a look.'

As he stooped down by the carriage, a dark, fast-moving blur behind where he had been standing caught my eye as a crow alighted onto a large rock that people often used as a resting place on their way up the hill. It hopped from side to side on spindly legs to appraise me through one black eye, the other appearing to have been plucked out quite recently, during a fight maybe. A thin tendril of something spilled out from the hole where it had once been. I looked away, suddenly nauseous.

'Horses are spooked.' The coachman stated, causing me to jump in my seat. I turned to see him standing upright alongside the carriage again. 'No getting them to go any further, I can tell you that.'

'I'll walk from here.' I told him. 'Return to the Inn and wait for me there.'

The coachman nodded and reached to open the door. 'Sir.'

Elizabeth's grave was towards the back of the churchyard, where all the newest ones were. As I made my way towards it in the dying light, I passed the resting place of Martha, Elizabeth's closest friend and the first to succumb to the consumption which had eventually taken them both. The dirt on top of it was freshly turned over. I walked on, my stomach clenching around another wave of nausea.

As I neared Elizabeth's grave, I saw that standing beside it were one of my father's guards and the church watchman, who was holding a lamp. A large pile of earth had been crudely deposited behind them.

'What is the meaning of this?' I demanded, stepping forward into the lamplight. 'Who gave you permission to defile my wife's grave?'

The guard stepped forward, and though his eyes gleamed with intensity, the ridges of his face and the deep sockets of his eyes fell into shadow, giving him a grotesque appearance. 'Sir, the Baron...'

'Such nonsense I have never heard!'

'It is not nonsense sir, I beg you!' The watchman insisted, holding the lamp out in front of him like some sort of repellent. 'She is not the first! Look upon her and see for yourself. We cannot wait any longer. They are weak in the daylight, slow to awaken. But at night...' He trailed off as I took another step towards him.

'You have opened her coffin! I will have someone's head for what has been done here!'

'Sir.' The watchman implored me, raising the lamp so that it blazed in front of my face, hurting my eyes. 'You must look at her.'

'What are you saying? That she's some sort of... What? A Ghoul? A Vampire?' I swung my arm out to push the lamp away and he flinched, drawing backwards. 'Are you mad?'

'Not at all.' He told me somberly. 'I assure you of that. And once you see for yourself...' He licked his lips. 'The Baron said...'

I stared at him. 'What? That I would do my duty?'

'Yes.'

He flicked his gaze to the ground beside him where somebody had placed a large piece of wood whittled to a point, a hammer and an axe. 'She has knocked upon your father's door.' He went on.

'You know what that means.'

I wanted to hit him, to shake him until all the torment I was feeling somehow drained away. 'If that were true.' I told him, speaking slowly, trying and failing to keep my voice steady. 'You can be sure that I would indeed do my duty. But it is impossible! Lies! I cannot believe it.'

'You shall.'

He stepped back and walked around to the far side of Elizabeth's grave. It was the first time I had been able to bring myself to look down upon it. I saw that the coffin lid had been forced open and then placed back atop, loosely at an

Reply of the Soul to the Body.

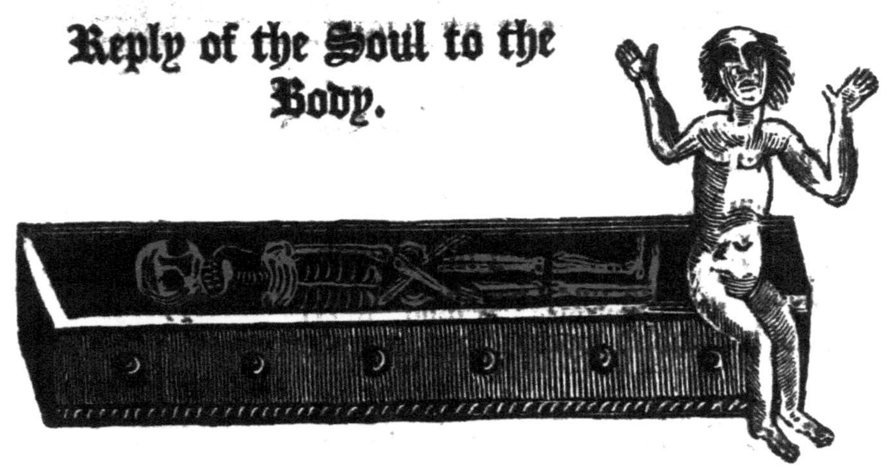

angle. My hands clenched into fists where they hung at my sides.

I turned my gaze back up toward the two men and they stared back at me. The churchyard darkened around us as dusk fell completely. The lamplight flickered and jumped over the space between us.

I dropped down into a sitting position by the hole in the ground, feeling the dank coldness of the soil seep through my breeches. Letting my legs fall over one side of the open grave, I used my arms to carefully lower myself down. The lid of the casket was almost split in two, I saw, as I positioned myself at the bottom end of the narrow space with my feet placed either side of the receptacle that contained what was left of my wife. Unnecessary force had obviously been used to loosen it. I leant forwards and gently pushed the lid to the side, closing my eyes as I did so. I heard movement from above and behind, as the watchman moved to illuminate what was in front of me with the lamp.

When I could bear the moment no more, I opened my eyes.

She lay there on her back as though she were just asleep. Her cheeks were flushed, her lips slightly parted, plump and dark, as though stained with strawberry juice or something similar. There was a sweet smell about her, slightly sickly.

'She lives.' I breathed, my heart thumping against my ribcage.

'She does not, sir.' The watchman's voice said quietly from above.

I ignored him and bent uncomfortably, turning my head sideways to place an ear against her chest. I discerned no movement. She did not seem to draw breath.

'You must raise her top lip, sir.' The voice came again.

'Pardon me?' I asked sharply.

'Her teeth.'

I reached a shaking hand to rest against her chin. Her skin felt smooth and cold against mine. Gently, with my forefinger and thumb, I raised her top lip.

'In the name of...'

I reeled back at the sight of the incisor that had seemed to draw down at my touch, lengthening before my eyes. In the flickering lamplight, I thought I saw her eyelashes twitch, as though she was about to wake up from a deep sleep. A trick of light, it must be!

'I can't believe it.' I breathed.

'Now you see what you must do.' The church watchman said.

The eyelashes flickered once more.

'...Yes.' I finally answered.

'I will pass down the stake and the hammer.' He told me.

I received them wordlessly.

'You must hammer in the stake.' He told me. 'Quickly, now. Then we will remove her head.'

I raised the stake above her chest, looking down at her. My vision blurred.

'I... I can't.' I lowered the stake.

'You must...'

'I mean, I can't do it by myself. My hands... they're shaking.'

There was a scuffle, as the guard lowered himself down to stand facing me, feet either side of the top of the coffin, and Elizabeth's face.

'You hold the stake and I'll hammer it down.' He told me.

I nodded. Then I dropped the stake and swung the hammer at him as hard as I could.

He made an 'oof' sound as the hammer connected with his shoulder. The blow had knocked me off balance and he was upon me before I could even begin to right myself. Within a second he had knocked the hammer out of my hand, spun me around and was using his weight to press my body into the wall of dirt that lined the bottom end of the grave. I'd never really had a chance, I consoled myself, as I began to choke on the earth which was filling my mouth and nostrils. He was a trained guard, after all.

There was a dull, thudding sound as his weight suddenly left me. I fell backwards, gasping and was violently bumped into from behind, propelled forwards into the dirt wall again. I heard wet gurgling sounds emanating from behind me and the sound of fast fading footsteps from above. My nose throbbing with pain, I reached up, clutching at soil and grass, using the last of the strength in my arms and legs to pull myself upwards and out, rolling my body over to come to rest on my back in the dirt beside the grave. I stared up at the newborn stars, sucking in deep breath after deep breath, waiting for my racing heartbeat to slow. All around me was silent now.

Eventually, I shakily rose to a standing position, looking around for the watchman. He was nowhere to be seen.

I turned and looked down.

A pale hand, smeared with a glistening, dark substance emerged from the open grave, fingers

clenching against the soil. As I watched, this was followed by another, as Elizabeth began to pull herself out of the place where I had witnessed her burial, weeks before.

I swayed in front of her as she rose, her black hair dulled with dirt, her eyes flashing silver in a face streaked with a substance that I didn't want to think too much about. She came to me, pressing her body against my own and I could feel my heart beating against the hollow void of her chest. I buried my fingers into her dry, knotted hair, feeling clumps of it coming away in my hands. Something skittered over my wrist, disappearing up my sleeve. She nestled her face into the space between my shoulders and neck, inhaling raggedly.

We had promised to love and protect each other, always. I had failed in my duty to keep that promise, but I had been given another chance. Nothing else mattered now.

'Elizabeth, my love.' I whispered. 'I've come home.'

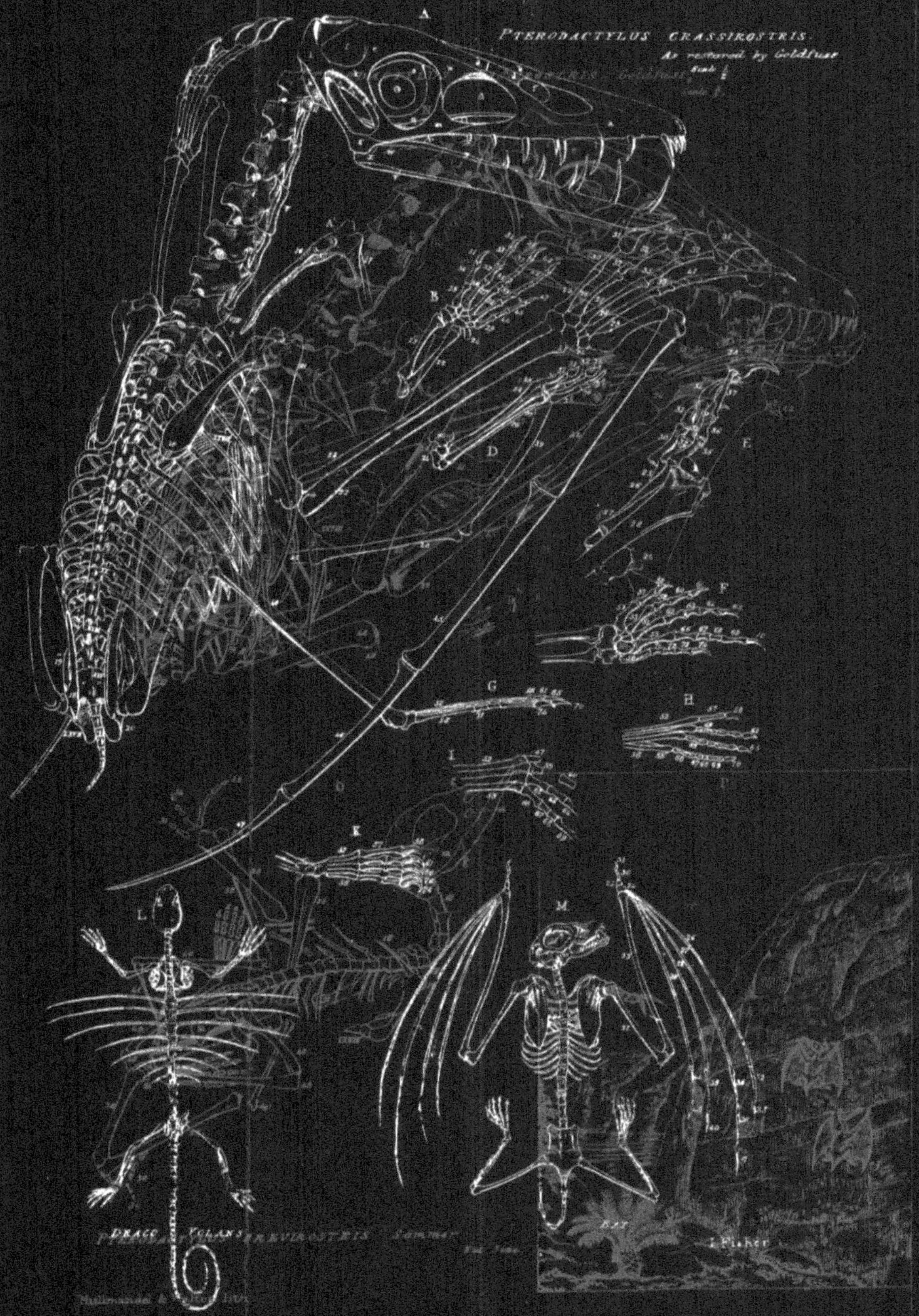
PTERODACTYLUS CRASSIROSTRIS.
As restored by Goldfuss

REBECCA PARFITT has worked in publishing for over a decade. By day, she is Commissioning Editor for Honno — the UK's longest running women's press; by night she haunts the desk at Ghastling Towers. She is a writer, editor and director. Her first short film, *Feeding Grief to Animals*, was commissioned and produced by the BBC and FfilmCymru Wales. She is currently working on a horror screenplay and a book of macabre short stories for which she won a Writers' Bursary from Literature Wales. Two stories from this collection were published in *The New Gothic Review* in 2020. *rebeccaparfitt.com*

TRACEY REES is an aspiring writer of short stories and poetry and works as an editor for an online medical education provider. Tracey joined *The Ghastling* team as an editorial assistant in 2022. She lives with her husband and two feline friends near the whispering woods in South Wales, where she can often be found seeking out nocturnal animals for morbid conversations during her bouts of insomnia. When not busy doing those things Tracey is passionate about classic horror movies, spooky tales, travelling, drinking tea, and rearranging the furniture.

JEN SMITH-FURMAGE is *The Ghastling*'s social media and marketing manager, a freelance publishing person, and feminist educator. Like most millennial horror fans, she started reading Stephen King at an inappropriately early age and now worships at the altar of Shirley Jackson, Catriona Ward and Mike Flanagan. Jen lives in South West England (she could probably throw you to Avebury Stone Circle from her house) with her black pug and brood of unruly children.

ANDREW ROBINSON is a printmaker and graphic designer. A self-taught artist specialising in linocut prints, his interests and influences stem from wildlife, printed ephemera, mythology, and all things creepy or otherworldly. Andrew inhabits the eastern woods of Canada with his partner and two daughters. *monografik.ca*

FAWN EMMALEE WARD is a copywriter, editor and author based in the Pacific Northwest in the US. She strives to create emotional work with a strong sense of place that roots readers in experience and memory. Her work has been featured in the *Reed College Creative Review* and *Pinhole Poetry*.

ASHLEY HARNETT lives in London where he spends his evenings reading to indulge a life-long fascination with the weird and the gothic. He occasionally writes his own tales.

MAT TROY is a Cardiff-based writer & performer. Some of his projects to date include co-writing the paranormal comedy drama *Agents of L*O*V*C*R*A*F*T*, which reached the finals of the UK Sitcom trials; *Dust and Dandruff*, a bio-play of the poets Ivor Cutler and Phyllis King; and his first poem in Welsh which was displayed in an exhibition at Dinefwr National Trust estate. As well as previous issues of *The Ghastling*, Mat has also been published in *Neon Literary, Just Snails! surreal fiction, the ASP journal* and the inaugural issue of Carrion Press magazine *Decay*. Mat is a sketch writer for *Welcome Strangers* on BBC Radio Wales. His current project, an episode of the detective audio drama series Aniline City, called *True Crime* is due to be released this spring.

SIMON JOHN PARKIN is a graphic designer by trade, living in Somerset with his partner and son. He has previously been published in *The Ghastling*. He has self-published a non-fiction book, *The Sunrise Swim Club*, about the twelve monthly sunrise swims he and his family did on the easing of lockdown. Currently, he is working towards completing a book of supernatural short stories set in a tower block in his home town of Dudley.

CHARLOTTE TURNBULL's work was published as part of the Galley Beggars Short Story Prize 2023, and appears in many other places, including *Litro, New England Review, Weird Horror* and *Nightjar Press*.

KATHERINE STANSFIELD is a multi-genre novelist and poet. Her historical crime series *Cornish Mysteries* has won the Holyer and Gof Fiction Prize and been shortlisted for the Winston Graham Memorial Prize. The most recent instalment is *The Mermaid's Call*. She co-writes a fantasy crime trilogy with her partner David Towsey, publishing as D. K. Fields, and has also published two full length poetry collections and a pamphlet with Seren. Katherine is co-editor, with Caroline Oakley, of *Cast a Long Shadow*: new crime short stories by women writers from Wales, published by Honno. She teaches creative writing for Faber Academy and has been a Royal Literary Fund Fellow. She lives in Cardiff.

ALEX GILLINDER is a horror obsessive who hopes to one day work as a comic writer/illustrator. They have previously had work published in *The Ghastling*, and they haunt the North East area with their partner and two cats.

EMMA OXLEY lives in Sheffield, where she divides her spare time between writing, walking and daydreaming. She is currently working on her first novel.

HANNAH DURHAM is an illustrator & printmaker based in Wales. She runs *a studio, somewhere* and creates bold, colourful art inspired by nature and life. Her work can be viewed *@astudiosomewhere* and *astudiosomewhere.com*

fig. 2362